CW00762175

THE PRIMITIVES

A NOVEL

BY
DARLENE BARRY QUAIFE

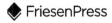 FriesenPress

One Printers Way
Altona, MB R0G 0B0
Canada

www.friesenpress.com

Copyright © 2024 by Darlene Barry Quaife
First Edition — 2024

Author Photograph: Jaz Hart

Cover Illustration: "Cave Art" painting by Darlene Barry Quaife

The Primitives" is a work of fiction. All incidents and dialogue, all characters with exception of historical facts and well-known historical figures, are the product of the author's imagination and are not to be construed as real. Where real-life historical figures appear, the situations, incidents, and dialogues concerning those persons are entirely fictional and are not intended to depict actual events or to change the entirely fictional nature of the work.

ISBN
978-1-03-830381-3 (Hardcover)
978-1-03-830380-6 (Paperback)
978-1-03-830382-0 (eBook)

1. FIC014080   FICTION, HISTORICAL, 20TH CENTURY

Distributed to the trade by The Ingram Book Company

ALSO BY
DARLENE BARRY QUAIFE

Novels
Bone Bird
Days And Nights On the Amazon
Polar Circus
Wildnis

Graphic NonFiction
Death Writes: A Curious Notebook

REVIEWS OF
PREVIOUS NOVELS

"*Bone Bird* is an ambitious first novel which combines the tactile reality of life in a rain-drenched, dying logging town with the empowering female spirit – not only of native myth, but of suffering, surviving peoples from around the world. Darlene Barry Quaife brings a new and distinctive voice and vision to our literature." - *Jane Rule, author*

"A provocative, richly satisfying narrative tapestry." *The Globe and Mail (Bone Bird)*

"As we read this far-seeing novel (*Bone Bird*), we can see that instead of staking our territory, we should be sharing our cultures. Quaife accomplishes this with vivid detail, pithy dialogue, and a deft blending of realism and imagination. - *Mollie Hooper, CM Archive*

"As she demonstrated in *Bone Bird,* Darlene Barry Quaife is a writer of wit and courage. In this her second novel, *Days & Nights on the Amazon*, she charts dangerous lives and follows a cunning river in a fine demonstration of her passion for life and true poetic vision." - *Rachel Wyatt, playwright & novelist*

"A river-run tale (*Days & Nights on the Amazon*), narrated by the Amazon herself. A dog who prefers electrical outlets to sunbeams. And a woman, whose 'road trip' adventure depends solely on the river's whispered dreams of seduction and escape. This is a strange and compelling story." - *Peter Oliva, novelist*

Dedicated to Ron

EPIGRAPH

Who are the Primitives?
The Prehistoric peoples who left a legacy of Cave Art.
Or
20th Century European Fascists who left a legacy of
violent destruction?

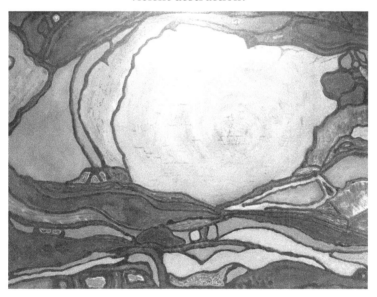

Light Beyond The Cave, a painting by Darlene Barry Quaife

PREFACE

Dedicated to the Mackenzie-Papineau "Mac-Paps" Battalion of Canadian volunteers fighting for democracy in the Spanish Civil War, July 17, 1936 to October 29, 1938. And to Jean Watts, the first woman Mac-Paps brigader, journalist, and ambulance driver.

Dedicated to Dorothy Livesay, poet and activist; P.K. Page, poet, painter, and diplomat; Sheila Doherty Watson, writer and educator, for contributions to the creation of Canadian Culture. According to Max Wyman in his book *The Compassionate Imagination*: "the arts are central to a functioning democracy."

Right Hand Left Hand Dorothy Livesay

Journey With No Maps P. K. Page

always someone to kill the doves Sheila Doherty
(Watson)

TIME & PLACE
The Spanish Civil War
September 1936 to January 1937

PROLOGUE

THE RAIN IN SPAIN

Serra de San Mamede, Galicia

The shepherd's hut is surprisingly snug. A torrential rain, yet nothing drips from the slate roof onto their army surplus blankets. The beating of the rain hides the sounds of sleep. Shale assumes the others are sleeping while she worries about the trail turning into a mire. As if the going isn't hard enough on this mountain. The trail is steep. Shale wonders yet again why she has brought these women here? Assistants, yes, she needed help to quickly document the cave. But what was she thinking recruiting these women, these Canadians that she met in a London pub? She gives her head a shake. Their only credentials are that they can hold their liquor and can sing a passable rendition of *Pennies From Heaven*. And the cave . . . what if the cave has flooded? She doesn't know. She hasn't worked on the site during the wet season. The risk, the danger could all be in vain. Needs must during war.

Sheila hears the rain of her childhood . . . coastal rain is never soft, never forgiving. Unlike the rain of her home in the Cariboo . . . desert rain that slakes the land and the mind.

London rain, Pat thinks. She just got used to London rain and now she's in the mountains of Spain. The rain in Spain – a silent sigh – how is it she's here and not on the plain?

Rain in the mountains is a shape-shifter. It may be snow by morning. Born in a prairie blizzard makes Dorothy an expert on the two faces of rain.

I

INQUISITION

El Castillo, Galicia

I

INQUISITION

Blindfolded, led upstairs, down corridors and into a room the fug of which causes an unbidden image to appear behind her darkened lids: She is a child entering a bunkhouse used by the men digging fossils out of Mount Field. There stands Mr. Walcott's daughter, Helen, examining a piece of shale. She licks the stone and holds it out. Helen's tongue has revealed a mysterious creature. Young Grace is so entranced by the fossil that Mr. Walcott nicknames her "Shale" and puts her to work.

The blindfold removed, she is deposited like an articulated mannequin in a high-backed wooden chair. From behind a ponderous antique desk comes a voice.

"You are a stranger, a foreigner. You have no right to be here."

"I'm here in the name of science—"

"What science could possibly bring you to Galicia? And you a woman."

The science of humankind—"

"Do you take me for a fool?"

"Archaeology . . . the study of the ancients. Surely, you are aware of Spain's caves, the rock art of Cantabria?"

He comes from behind the desk to tower over her. "Women are not scientists."

"Women are many things. My assistants are writers and artists. I assure you I am an accredited archaeologist. I am Dr. Grace Clifden."

"You are my prisoner. A spy. That is your truth. Now I want the facts. And you will give them to me . . . you and your friends."

Shale can't help but laugh.

He slaps her face. A quick, efficient stroke that leaves the imprint of his ornate ring on her cheek. "You are in possession of maps."

Steadying herself and in her best professorial voice, she answers, "Copies of Spanish maps housed in the—"

"Be that as it may, the originals are not covered in ciphers; yours are."

"Archaeological notations in Pitman's business shorthand. Nothing more."

"You would have me believe that you have come here in a time of war to study the caves? No one is that foolhardy, not even a foreigner."

"Your civil war is a threat to your heritage."

"What? Those crude paintings? That is not Spanish heritage. We did not descend from primitives."

"Perhaps not directly—"

"It is all just a hoax . . . those cave paintings . . . someone's idea of a joke. You know it and I know it. So, I will ask you again, who are you spying for? Who sent you?"

"This is absurd. You have no right to keep us here." She rises from the chair.

He pushes her back down, pulls a dagger from his belt, and pins her right hand to the heavy wooden arm of the chair, the blade between her middle fingers—the hilt and fear holding her hand in place. Her face bloodless, her only thought is for her three assistants, women she had persuaded to her cause—yes, her cause, not theirs.

This is a rock-hard country. Everything made of stone.

"Your boss says you are an artist, but I know better. It is obvious: a real artist would not spend his time copying crude paintings made by inept children."

"Beauty is in the eye of the beholder."

"Too clever for your own good."

"Why have you abducted us? What do you want?"

"I will ask the questions, not you. Abduct, no. Arrest, yes."

"We have committed no crime."

"You are a spy. What is your real name?"

"P.K. Page."

"That is not a name. An alias, and not even a good one."

"Patricia Katherine Page."

"Proof." He slams his fist down on the desk. "Where are your papers?"

The prearranged lie. "In our pensión of course. We would not carry something so important into the field."

"What field? You were apprehended in the mountains."

"The archaeological field of study—"

"Lies. All lies. My men searched the pensión. No papers. None for any of you."

"Well, then, they were overlooked or stolen."

"Thieves," he roars. "You call us thieves."

"No, that's not—"

"No. Well, I'll show you how we deal with liars." He presses her right wrist down hard against the wooden arm of the chair and secures it there with a leather strap that dangles from the underside. Doing the same with the left, he expects her to struggle. Instead she lifts her head and fixes her eyes on a point beyond him. Is this courage or shock? He cannot tell.

She will not be intimidated by stone walls. Her eyes dart everywhere.

This annoys him. He grabs the discarded blindfold.

When he touches her face, she goes perfectly still, the way some animals do. He is gratified by this. As he ties the black linen scarf over her eyes, he thinks— being sightless, perhaps this one will tell the truth.

"Who sent you here?" A direct question, a direct answer. To hell with all the denials.

"Sent? I don't know what? I came of my own free will."

"You came freely to spy. Yes, yes but for whom? Who is your master?"

"I belong to no one but myself."

"Enough of this. Tell me what I want to know or I will give you a lesson in free will."

"You want what I don't have. How can I tell you what I don't know?"

"Liar," he shouts in her face. "Spy."

"I am none of those things. I am Sheila Doherty, schoolmistress."

"César." It is a command. The mastiff rises. "Come." The great, black dog appears from behind the ornate desk. Like all of his breed, his panting is louder than his footfall.

Sheila screams.

In turn, man and dog go perfectly still. The stillness of the hunter. "Stand down."

The mastiff returns to his place behind the desk.

The man pours water from a pitcher over the woman languishing in a believable faint.

"At ease." He leaves the room knowing that César is inspecting the liar.

When the dog puts a paw gently on Sheila's knee, she removes the blindfold, opens one eye and smiles. Reaching for the huge black head, she strokes César's ears and gives him a heartfelt hug. Sheila whispers into his fur, "You knew along, didn't you? You great bear of a dog."

The last of the four prisoners. He had decided to have her escorted to his office and left there in the company of César. Fifteen minutes should be enough. He doesn't want another fainting episode.

He opens the door smartly, expecting to find the woman cowering in a corner. Instead, she is standing at the window, looking out, with her hand caressing the silky black ears of the dog sitting beside her. Neither dame nor dog moves when he enters.

"César," he says through clenched teeth. These recalcitrant women have frayed his patience beyond repair. Worst still, his loyal companion is bewitched. "Stand down."

He points at the woman. "And you, sit."

César retreats to his place.

Without a glance at the room or the man, she occupies the chair behind the desk. Better placed to secret her fingers in the loose coat of the mastiff.

Apoplectic, for a moment it looks as if he will commit violence. Suddenly, he is gone.

Sometime later there is a firm knock at the door, followed by the entrance of a man in a black cassock. "I am Father Francisco."

She extends her hand across the desk. "Dorothy Livesay, kidnapped Canadian."

He locks his hands behind his back and crosses to the window. "You have chosen a very bad time to visit Spain. No doubt you were aware of the conflict here, and yet you came. This is surprising behaviour, indeed. Hardly prudent. Highly suspicious."

"Suspicious? Four women documenting prehistoric cave art in the mountains? We came to preserve history."

"Why here? Why now?"

"There is a need. When men war, nothing is sacred."

"Sacred?" Finally, he turns from the window to look at her. "Pagan drawings? Deluded. You and your friends are mad."

2

BE BRAVE

El Castillo, Galicia

2

BE BRAVE

She must find a way to reach the others. Get them out of this mess. How could she be so irresponsible! Putting these women in danger. They have no stake in this; they're not even archaeologists. Shale scrapes the stone floor hard with the trowel. Black flakes fly up in her face. Suddenly she realizes she shouldn't be inhaling this crud. Looking around the corridor, she notices that the stone walls glisten with moisture. And where the walls meet the floor, there are trails worn in the encrustation she has been ordered to scrape off the floor. Rats, she thinks. She's disturbing and breathing in black mold and rat shit. Immediately, Shale reaches for the bandana at her neck, loosens it, and pulls it up over her mouth and nose. How to warn the others? She's sure they also will be made to do this demeaning work. The commandant, or whatever he calls himself, is trying to show them who is boss. He's started with her, since she is the nominal leader of this field crew.

Knowing that she's being watched, Shale scrapes and thinks. The trowel is surprisingly sharp; obviously, the guards don't see her as a threat. Well, she knows from experience a trowel can become a weapon when confronting thieves on a dig. Robbed of her freedom here, yes, but she can put this tool to work for her. Surreptitiously she carves letters into what could be a centuries old patina:

BE BRAVE
COVER NOSE & MOUTH WITH BANDANA
DON'T LET THEM SEE

Shale stands and stretches, as if her back aches. She assesses her inscription. It is as she hoped: dim light and distance reduces the letters to scuffs. On their hands and knees, the women will see it.

Hearing movement along the corridor, Shale returns to her task. There are two-legged rats approaching.

Back in her cell—and it is a real cell in a real dungeon she reminds herself because she still can't believe it—Shale attempts to clean her hands in the wooden bucket filled with water meant for sluicing the piss pot. Trying without success to get her nails clean, she senses she is being watched.

In one quick, fluid movement she is at the grill in the door, eye to eye with her watcher. Startled, the intruder's eyes appraise, then crinkle at the corners in amusement. Shale cocks her head, and leaves the door.

It is opened by a stranger, perhaps a new guard. Then she looks again. Tall and thin, he could be one of her colleagues from the Universitat de València.

For a moment she believes the nightmare has ended. The commandant has contacted the university, as she suggested, and they have sent a representative. "Who are you?"

"Dr. Castro, at your service."

"I do not need a doctor. I am not unwell."

"You misunderstand me, Dr. Clifden. I am a doctor of psychology."

"Neither am I insane. Anger is a sensible emotion under the circumstances. And I am angry."

"I can well imagine."

"That I am angry or insane?"

His smile is inward, perhaps, in response to her raised eyebrow. "Certainly indisposed. Shall we begin again? I have been directed to speak with you."

"Directed—by our abductor, I take it. Why did the commandant ask you?"

Tickled by her appellation, Dr. Castro tries to appear aloof, "El

Comandante, as you say, is my brother, Octavio Leonidas Castro. You are a guest in our ancestral home."

This elicits as outright guffaw from Shale. "Your hospitality leaves something to be desired." She looks over his shoulder to the door. "My question still stands—why you?"

"I speak English. I am told you are Canadian?"

"Yes, as are my companions. We are in your country to complete a field study."

"Rather bad timing, don't you think?"

"This work cannot wait."

"And your colleagues feel the same way, given the circumstances?"

"Firstly, they are not colleagues. That is—they are not archaeologists. My companions are writers and artists. Given the circumstances, as you say, they agreed to help me document a recent discovery."

"An unusual field crew. Hardly seems cogent. Surely, you can see why my brother might have his suspicions? Especially, since you can prove none of this—not even your identity."

Shale holds his gaze. "There is proof to be had. As easy as a phone call to Professor Luis Gonzalvo at the Universitat de València. Professor Gonzalvo has authorized my work in Spain. He knows me well. We have worked together on other sites over the years."

It is clear that her inquisitor is assessing her. "If I may say so, you seem rather young to find yourself a professional of standing."

"And you neglected to add—'a woman.' I have been doing field work since I was six years old. My patron and mentor was an eminent administrator of the Smithsonian Institution in Washington, DC. You may have heard of it."

"Indeed, I studied at Harvard, as it happens."

"Ah, Veritas. So, what is the present truth?"

He studies her closely before answering, "My brother is ambitious."

Shale registers the change in the man before her. His truth looms large, burdened with meaning. Her adoptive brothers taught her to play chess. What is the game? Who is to be sacrificed in this gambit?

Dr. Castro turns to leave.

"What do you propose to do?" Shale asks.

"Talk to your companions."

"Why?"

"I've been charged to do so."

He walks down the corridor, noting that his brother has isolated the women one from another. He is reminded of an old trick from childhood that he and his brother devised to individualize the family servants. When a new one arrived, the brothers surreptitiously hung a piece of cutlery from the domestic's bedroom door. For obvious reasons, a knife signaled danger; a fork was for an all-seeing, piercing person; a soup spoon denoted a jolly sort, round and nourishing; a teaspoon, on the other hand, suggested a small-minded individual; and on it went.

Dr. Castro stops in front of a cell door from which hangs a butter knife. A dark-haired woman sits cross-legged on the bunk, eyes closed, palms pressed together before her face not in prayer it would seem, but to monitor her breathing. Ah, yes, his brother has decided she is smoothly decisive, unlike Dr. Clifden, who, as he looks back along the corridor, rates a carving knife.

Before he interviews another of these women, he decides to walk the length of the damp corridor to discover what other implements are missing from his brother's kitchen. Two more cells down and he finds a fork. Indeed, what does a Canadian fork look like? He peers in and is accosted by dark eyes on the other side of the grill. Pierced by her eyes, his hand tightens on what he thinks is the door handle, but in reality is the handle of the fork.

Without a word between them, Dr. Castro moves on. He sees the hook before he reaches the worm-eaten oak door. It stops him. Is this symbol about the woman in the cell, or is it about him? Hooks— hooks used to hang dead fowl from the kitchen beams—the hooks of his childhood nightmares.

Dr. Castro takes a deep breath and slides back the bolt. Before he can reach for the handle, the door swings out with force, knocking him to the filthy floor. What appears to be a boy leaps over him, running down the corridor and calling for Shale, Dorothy, Pat.

Before he can pull himself together and make it to his feet, she has released the fork and is descending on the butter knife.

He sprints for the carving knife, the real weapon. Pulling it from the door, he turns on the prisoners.

"Who are you?" the fork demands.

"Your confessor—"

"He's the brother," Shale says through the grill in her cell door. "The commandant's brother."

"What do you want?" The hook glares at him. Not a boy after all.

"Some fresh air," he says. "Will you accompany me to the courtyard?" He keeps his eyes on the women while releasing the bolt on the carving knife's door. Then he points to the stairs at the end of the corridor.

The door at the top of the stairs opens to a sun that is friend and foe: beatific light that disorients.

Dr. Castro leads them to a bench under a colonnade. "Shall we begin again? I am Dr. Alexandre Sebastián Castro, professor of psychology at the University of Madrid. And, yes, I am also the brother."

They look at him expectantly, study him with cautious interest.

"What does the commandant want?" Shale asks pointedly.

"In today's Spain, I would say power. It is no longer enough to be a big fish in a small pond. The waves of war have turned all that we know into flotsam. We now live in abject fear. It brings out the worst in all of us."

"And what is the worst your brother can do?" Having done fieldwork in various foreign countries, Shale is fully aware that their situation is precarious. Foreign fieldwork depends primarily on goodwill, which is glaringly absent in a Spain she no longer recognizes.

"Forget what it is to be human." His gaze takes in the courtyard where once two boys pretended to be crusaders.

"And what of Madrid?" Dorothy asks.

"I am here." Dr. Castro's eyes remain on the courtyard where the earth is scorched by an unforgiving sun.

"You escaped the battle." Dorothy probes.

"I escaped tyranny, inside and outside of University City."

"Go on," Shale says quietly.

He turns to look at her, at them. "The Republican government wanted to turn me into Torquemada."

"The Grand Inquisitor?" Pat offers, looking confused.

"The State Intelligence Service tried to coerce me, and for that matter, my colleagues, into devising programs of psychological torture." He shakes his head. "What I witnessed was Lewis guns in the main hall of the red brick Philosophy and Letters Building, and the campus a no man's land. And on the road to El Escorial . . . the Moors, brought in from Africa by the Nationalists, charging head-on the big guns of the Republican Army. There were so many bodies . . . they were piled up and burned. The smell . . . .."

They sit in silence. No birds sing, as if they too are appalled by war.

"Civil war, the devils within," Dorothy says barely above a whisper.

"You do not strike me as women possessed by demons, so why—"

"We are believers," is Dorothy's unbidden answer. "We believe in the power of knowledge."

"Art, artifact, ritual define us." Shale nods. "To know that we are more than the power-mongers would have us believe is to cut the puppet strings." Shale's hands will not be still. "To understand that we have been evolving for thousands upon thousands of years is to recognize the value of each and every human being. The prehistoric caves confirm that we are more."

"And more than ever, we need to know who and what we are." Small though she may be, Sheila challenges him with flashing eyes. "You of all people should understand that."

Rather than be turned to stone by her Medusa gaze, Dr. Castro stands, walks away and beckons them to follow. Yes, he has been put to rout, but with a purpose. They have about them the scent of the sacred pneuma of Delphi.

To the dismay of the women, they return inside. Rather than down, they climb up stairs and are led to a second-floor room.

"I present the gallery: the repository of my grandfather's loot. Specifically, his collection of kraters. He was an amateur archaeologist of the Heinrich Schliemann School of self-designated antiquarians. He had a fascination for the Oracle at Delphi and the Gorgon."

The women, led by Shale, move into a high-ceilinged room, heavily draped. Dr. Castro strides across Persian carpets to throw back brocade curtains. Light floods in, revealing bedazzled visitors staring at museum-quality display cases.

"Surely these are replicas?" Shale turns suspicious eyes on him.

"No replicas. My grandfather was a true collector."

"Not only is this krater massive, it's Greek from the classical period." Shale circles the pedestal displaying a metal vessel that stands at least five feet in height. "And it's bronze. Unbelievable. Very few have survived. The metal was reused, melted down, while the handles were often kept as ornaments. You can see why. Look at the exquisite figures that make up these volute handles."

Dr. Castro issues a polite laugh. "Exquisite. Surely not the Gorgon."

The others gather around to have a closer look.

Shale runs a finger down a smooth serpentine body. "Her arms are graceful, as are her snakes. She is balanced by a rampant lioness. And she has Athena's flashing eyes. As apotropaic symbols go, our Gorgon is regal."

"You seem to have overlooked the protruding tongue." Dr. Castro manages a grimace.

"Not at all. That is her power. How else to ward off the evil eye?"

"Apotropaic?" Sheila seems to be in a staring match with the wide eyes of the Gorgon head.

"A lucky charm," Dorothy offers.

Shale nods. "Ancient Greece and beyond. Medusa and her sisters. The snakes, especially those that make up her hair, can be traced back to the dragon Delphyne, protecting the priestess Pythia at Delphi."

Dorothy takes one last look at the krater and makes for the bookshelves lining the wall near the door.

Dr. Castro is on alert until he sees her studying the shelves. Sheila joins her, running an index finger down spines and asking Dorothy if she reads French, German, Italian, Spanish?"

Having set the scene, successfully he thinks, Dr. Castro leaves the women, suggesting he will look for his grandfather's journals in a leather-covered desk commanding the room from a corner by the window. Not so far away that Dr. Castro cannot eavesdrop on the women's various conversations. In fact, the desk was purposely placed: the walls funneling sound to the corner.

What filters through to him as he opens and closes drawers is that Miss Livesay is fluent in French and Italian, while acquainted with German and Spanish. Miss Doherty has taught German to high school students. The women are familiar with the works of Dr. Freud and the Frankfurt School, and certainly, the American Behaviourists: his classmate at Harvard, B.F. Skinner, and the infamous John Broadus Watson.

"The fruit doesn't fall far from the tree," Dorothy whispers just loud enough for him to hear.

He chooses to remain with his head down, rummaging through a drawer, seemingly oblivious.

"Some familiar names on these shelves." When Sheila recognizes an author, she touches the spine. "My childhood home was the New Westminster Hospital for the Insane." Sheila caresses another book.

Dorothy gives her a sideways glance. "Good hospital, I'd say. You seem perfectly sane to me."

"Appearances can be deceiving." Sheila imitates the Gorgon by sticking out her tongue. "My father, the Doctor, was head of the Hospital. Our family lived in a tower on the hospital grounds."

Sheila steps back to get a better view of the top shelf near the ceiling. She knows from childhood experience that top shelves hold forbidden fruit. "Did you always want to be a writer, Dorothy?"

"Bred in the bone. My father and mother are both writers, always have been."

"Your father is some bigwig—"

"I don't know about that." Dorothy grins at the thought of what her father would think of the word *bigwig*. No doubt he would scoff at it. "He's general manager of The Canadian Press." Her tone is matter-of-fact.

Dr. Castro turns his attention to a chest standing behind his grandfather's desk. This change in position allows him to watch and listen as Dr. Clifden and Miss Page move among the artifacts.

"This is a most strange collection, don't you think?" Pat examines a gold torc. Not a particularly attractive piece of jewellery, in her opinion. "Look here, I wouldn't be caught dead wearing this hunk of gold in any century."

"It's Galician," is Shale's response.

"Yes?" Pat looks bewildered.

"From around here. Early Bronze Age—Celtic."

"Celts here?" Pat is beyond bewilderment.

"It's believed they were part of an early migration out of Eastern Europe."

"My God, what are these doing here?" Pat peers into a tray displaying arrowheads. "I used to find these when we went camping."

Shale looks over Pat's shoulder at obsidian points. Definitely Native North American. "Camping? Where?"

"South of Calgary. My father was a major in the Lord Strathcona's Horse. The regiments got together in the summer to train. And my mother set up housekeeping in a tent nearby."

"You grew up in Alberta?"

"We lived in Calgary for a short time on two occasions. My father was posted here and there in Canada."

Shale elaborates on her interest, "I was sent to school in Calgary—St. Hilda's School for Girls."

Pat wheels around. "No. It can't be. When? What years?"

"After my mother died. I was eight years old. I had been schooled at home in Field. My dad couldn't be father and mother." Shale looks away.

"I entered Grade One in 1923," Pat offers.

"Ah, you're a young one. I would have graduated from high school by then."

"Field? In British Columbia?"

"Yes, small railroad town. My father was a mechanic."

"Field. A long way from prehistoric caves—"

"Not as far as you might think. I met my first fossil when I was six years old. Helen Walcott stuck out her tongue, licked a rock, and uncovered a world with her spittle. Then she shoved it in my face for me to wonder at." Shale assesses Pat for signs of interest. She wasn't about to waste her story on the incurious.

"Do tell." Pat's large dark eyes have come to rest on Shale.

"Charles D. Walcott, fourth secretary of the Smithsonian Institution, uncovered the most important Cambrian fossil beds to date. And he did so above my hometown on the ridge between Mount Field and Mount Wapta. Mrs. Walcott and their sons worked on the site quarrying the shale, splitting, trimming, and packing the fossils for the trip down the mountain. My father was hired to help haul the crates to an old railroad bunkhouse near the Field train station. Helen Walcott and I worked in the bunkhouse, cleaning specimens. This is how I spent my summer holidays."

"Cambrian?" a single word from Pat.

"Geological time . . . 541 to 485 million years ago."

"Holy smoke!" Pat is wide-eyed.

"Yes, a considerable time before the Vatican used smoke signals."

"Wait a minute. You said quarrying shale. Is that where—"

"My name comes from? Properly speaking, my nickname, but yes. Bestowed on me by Mr. Walcott because I loved to lick life into the fossils."

"Charming," said with a grimace and then a smile.

"More than a passing childhood fancy. The habit continued during my summers at the Smithsonian."

"You spent your summers in Washington, DC?"

"My father died in an accident while working on an engine in the train yard. I went to live with the Walcott family when I was twelve." Shale nods over her shoulder. "Do you think we should rescue Dr. Castro from his dreadful pantomime?"

The gallery door slams open. "What the hell are you doing?" El Comandante fills the doorway.

"Looking for grandfather's journals. Have you moved them? They're supposed to be in—"

"Journals, be damned. The prisoners—who gave you permission to remove them from the cells?"

"As a professional courtesy, I am introducing our guests to grandfather's Collection."

"Courtesy! Guests! Have you gone mad? These women are spies. And my prisoners." His bluster takes him across the room.

The brothers stare into each other's faces over a desk older than their grievances.

El Comandante raises his hand and snaps his fingers. Three men storm into the room, trying not to be seen gawking at the contents. "Cells, now."

The men grab the women brusquely.

"Enough." Dr. Castro's voice is dangerous with authority.

El Comandante's head snaps up, chin out, belligerence in every muscle.

"I will remove these ladies"— Dr. Castro rounds the desk— "and I will come back here to talk to you, brother."

"Escort them," El Comandante orders his men as he positions himself behind the desk.

"I'll return, Ocho." Dr. Castro throws this brother a look, a challenge.

"See that you do, little brother."

Octavio takes in the room, disgusted by the dusty books and piles of old junk. If it were not for his little brother, it all would have been sold off long ago. But they both know too well the dictates of their grandfather's and father's wills. Alexandre would have him before a judge faster than one can say "Xandre."

He is sitting on a pile of cash, resources he desperately needs to make a bid for a place as the regional chief of state in the new government. These spies will be his opening move, his offering to General Franco. The General's Nationalists may not be in Galicia yet, but it won't be long. And he'll be ready."

Octavio's eyes shift from the bookshelves to the door, where Alexandre leans against the frame watching him. "What did you think you were doing?"

"Research."

"You forget yourself, Xandre."

"I did only as you asked."

"I ordered you to interrogate the women, not host a tea party."

"Listen and learn."

"What took you so long getting back here?" Octavio is searching for another transgression.

"I made a telephone call to the Universitat de València."

"You did what?"

"I spoke with Luis Gonzalvo, professor of archaeology. He confirmed Dr. Clifden's credentials. She was given permission to document the cave art she discovered in Serra de San Mamede. He was also aware she was bringing field assistants."

"Doesn't matter. I have plans for them."

"Did you know that Dr. Clifden is from the Smithsonian Institute in America?"

"She said she was Canadian. There—a proven lie."

"Dr. Clifden is Canadian. According to Professor Gonzalvo, she studied in America. And was mentored by the head of the prestigious Smithsonian. As well, she is affiliated with Cambridge University in England."

"All the better."

"These women are Canadian, yes, with significant connections in their own country as well as Britain and America. You could cause an international furor, embarrassing Spain and us."

Octavio's laugh is not unlike the bark of his mastiff. "Embarrassment. What world are you living in, little brother?"

"One in which I expect my only brother to be an honourable man."

୨୨୨୨

Dorothy is on her knees. As soon as Dr. Castro left, the henchmen put them to work scraping sections of the floor. Her attention is arrested by strange lines scratched in the encrusted surface. She had not noticed them until she had been forced roughly to the flagstones. Words form. Surreptitiously, she glances around, then raises the bandana at her throat to cover the lower part of her face.

When Dorothy chances another look around, she sees that Shale also has her bandana raised. Dr. Clifden looks like a bandit and Dorothy smiles to herself under cloth that smells of her sweat and fear.

She continues to scrape until the guards have moved to the stairwell, to smoke and joke. They think she doesn't understand what they are saying, but a first-class honours in modern languages serves her well.

While they assault the female body in the name of humour, Dorothy scratches words in the detritus time has laid down:

FEAR DRIVES THE HUMAN ANIMAL
LOOK BEHIND THE EYES ALWAYS

The last three years as a Social Worker has taught her many life lessons. She has no illusions about the fight here in Spain, in Europe, at home in Canada. University had introduced her to Engels, Marx, and Emma Goldman. Social Work in Montreal, Toronto, and New Jersey seared her mind and soiled her heart with Depression poverty and the defiling of human dignity.

Dorothy glances at Shale again and knows why. Why she, Dorothy Livesay, has come to Spain as part of this unlikely crew. Shale is Jean Watts incarnate. Jean Watts . . . her brilliant, tempestuous, childhood friend, who is now driving ambulances for the International Brigades. Right here in Spain, on the front lines, of course. Knowing Jean was in Spain was the lure; stopping in at Canada House in London was the line and sinker for Dorothy. She would have been home by now from Geneva, from the World Congress of Youth Organizations, if she hadn't been reeled in by the promise of a free lecture at Canada House.

♋♋♋

Octavio surveys the gallery. "I'm going to clear out this room; sell it all."

"Why? To finance your delusions of grandeur?" Alexandre's voice hardens.

Octavio rises, startled by his brother's perceptiveness. He makes a sweeping gesture with his arms, "Junk. All of it. I've known it from the moment we were allowed to cross the threshold of the old man's sanctuary. The smell was a dead giveaway."

"Indeed. Given the fact that grandfather died in this room."

"Don't get smart with me. You even said so at the time."

"Even if I agreed to your plan, Ocho, there is no market right now inside Spain, or out. The world only cares about where it's going, not where it came from. Europe is arming itself to the teeth. Spain is stripping its museums, depositing its treasures in talc mines—"

"What of this Smithsonian? America is an ocean away."

"What of it? Your actions have already hurt your chances there. Do you really think Dr. Clifden will give you a glowing introduction?"

Octavio gives Alexandre an imperious look. All straight back and boot heels, he leaves the room.

♋♋♋

On her knees in the dungeon, it is obvious to Shale that Dorothy has read her message. And now it looks as if Dorothy is scratching one of her own. Since they are not allowed to speak to each other, this may prove useful.

'The Brother,' Dr. Castro, has given her hope—an intelligent, educated person. Still, it depends upon his relationship with El Comandante. There is no doubt they are very different people. How to appeal to Dr. Castro, if given the chance again, is the question. What of his time at Harvard? Who does she know? Is there, perhaps, someone they have in common?

The rhythm of her arms helps her focus her mind. Ah, yes, Mary, her Vassar sister. Surely, as an American trained psychologist, Dr. Castro knows the behaviourist, John B. Watson, and perhaps even, his colleague, Mary Cover Jones.

♋♋♋

Dr. Castro dismisses the guards, who hesitate, but only momentarily. They recognize authority in his bearing. He's a Castro after all.

"Come, come, the sunshine awaits," he calls down the staircase, littered in cigarette butts. He knows who will be cleaning those up, and it won't be the women.

"Just what the doctor ordered." Shale leads the way and gives him a bright smile.

The women find a tray of glasses and a pitcher sitting on the bench they had occupied early in the day. The sun has found its way behind the colonnade's outside wall, casting the courtyard in shadow.

Dr. Castro pours sangría from the pitcher and hands them each a glass. He raises his drink. "*Que vivas durante todos los dias de tu vida. Salud!*"

While Pat and Sheila raise their glasses to meet Dr. Castro's, Shale and Dorothy look on in consternation.

"Would you care to explain yourself?" Dorothy asks him.

"There is no irony in my meaning." He looks directly at Shale and Dorothy. "To fulfill the prophecy, we will need to work together."

"What prophecy?" Sheila demands.

"*May you continue to live all the days of your life,*" he says, raising his sanguine glass to the light.

"So there is a real threat to our lives?" Pat asks. There is no light, only a deep red in her glass.

"As there is to mine and to every man, woman, and child in my country. War is war, and it will reach us here in the north— sooner than later. My brother is counting on it. You are his tribute. An offering at the feet of the Nationalists." He steps away. "Please sit. We must appear at ease."

When they have created an acceptable tableau for the unseen watcher, Alexandre begins again, "You must understand my brother. He is first and foremost a Castro. Our line goes back to the Bronze Age Celts or so he believes. Fierce fighters, the Celts, men and women. But it is the Romans my brother identifies with. This was a land of hill forts when the Romans invaded. They called the fortifications, *castros.*"

For some unfathomable reason, all Shale can think is that life and death have forged links ever stronger than her Vassar sister and an appeal to an American education could have. Suddenly everything deemed civilized has been dispossessed.

"What do you propose?" Dorothy's tone suggests she is no stranger to the negotiation table.

"We convince my brother that you are even more valuable than he believes."

"Then surely, at all costs, he will not release us." Pat is bewildered, as are the others.

"No, he will keep you safe instead." Dr. Castro looks from one to the other.

"What of value do we have to offer?" Shale looks dubious.

"Prestige." Dr. Castro lets them think about this single word while he refills their glasses. "Your connections. Your families."

They are stunned into laughter.

"To you, they may seem rather ordinary. But, with a bit of polish, Miss Page's father is a high-ranking military officer; Miss Doherty's father was a revered doctor; Miss Livesay's father is an architect of public opinion; Dr. Clifden's mentor was the head of an influential institution."

"How do you know these things about us?" Pat asks.

"Because he listens, unlike his brother," Shale offers.

"So, are we to believe you have joined our ranks?" Sheila flashes him a look.

"I am his most precious pawn."

"Your brother would do that? Turn you over to the Fascists?"

"One way or another, yes."

Silence

"I will need to convince 'El Comandante,' our code name, perhaps, that my civilized methods of interrogation are success-ful. While you are eating your evening meal in the kitchen, I will secret notebooks and pencils in your cells, under each mattress. I wish you to write an elevated history of your families and your international connections."

"You expect us to use our imaginations?" Pat asks.

"Yes, you are writers, after all."

"Embroider the facts, not create fiction? I would imagine El Comandante has ways of checking." Dorothy does not think much of this idea.

"It goes without saying, this is our secret. Make sure the guards do not see what you are doing, or find the notebooks. If by bad luck they do, tell them to talk to me."

"And your response will be?" What is his endgame? Shale wonders.

"The truth. I've asked you to write about your lives as a form of therapy."

True to his word, after their silent, meager supper, the women find notebooks and pencils tucked up in their cots. Their excitement knows no measure. Their nights behind stout wooden doors, and between even thicker stone walls have been silent, lonely. The words they write will take them home to their families.

⚋⚋⚋

The next morning the women are escorted to the gallery, where they are issued feather dusters and cleaning rags. El Comandante is preparing his booty for the auction block. In the meantime, Dr. Castro collects the notebooks from the cells and joins the women in the gallery. He is hoping to have something effectual to eventually share with his brother.

The women don't disappoint. It would appear they have written well into the night. As he reads Dr. Clifden's notebook, an idea is forming. She calls herself 'The Smithsonian Child,' and there is an illustration, a drawing of a girl surrounded by shelves full of artifacts. Just as the artifacts have tags attached to them, the child wears a tag tied to her wrist.

Alexandre surveys the room where the women are wielding feather dusters as if doing battle. A legion of women warriors—he tries to hide his smile behind the notebook.

But it is the room he is interested in. He is trying to see it the way his brother does. Suddenly, it occurs to him: none of these precious items are safe. He saw piles of books burned at University

City in Madrid. His family treasures would appear as so much trash to vandals. And the vandals are coming, as they've always come.

He contemplates The Smithsonian Child. "*Bring me your treasures*," she says. Yes, my treasures and more. He must talk to Dr. Clifden, privately.

Dr. Castro crosses the room. "Dr. Clifden, will you join me at the desk?"

Shale senses urgency in his bearing. "Yes, of course."

Settled into the corner, he speaks of what he foresees, while Shale's eyes travel from display case to display case.

"My brother wants to sell everything he can from the gallery to finance his political ambitions. Obviously, there is no market in Spain." He pauses to search her face. "What if we convince him that the Smithsonian is the only possible buyer? Of course, you would have to be free to negotiate with your people." He watches as she reviews this strategy.

Finally, she says, "There are some genuinely important artifacts here. That is in our favour. My alma mater, Vassar College, has a fine library that is always expanding its collection."

Alexandre's face flushes with anticipation. "We may have found a way to secure our freedom."

"Let's not get ahead of ourselves. There is still the question of my research. The Smithsonian is funding me."

Some of the light goes out of Alexandre's face. He looks up and notices the women watching them. He shifts his gaze to the window. After some time, he says, "My brother, Octavio, will not release you unless there is money on the table."

"The Smithsonian is anticipating the documentation of my discovery. The Secretary considers this an unprecedented find. If that were not the case, I would not have come to Spain during this abominable time."

"What will it take to complete your fieldwork?"

"A minimum of three weeks to survey the cave system and document the wall art and complete sample excavations."

"I can most probably convince my brother that you cannot go to the Smithsonian empty-handed. You must complete the work they have contracted. In the meantime you would be willing to contact your superiors and develop their interest in the Castro Collection."

Shale studies him. "Feasible. But both you and I are going to have to be convincing. Easier for me, perhaps, because I believe there are worthy items to recommend this collection. I will need documentation, of course. Your grandfather's journals might be acceptable. I read Spanish well enough to do the research, with a little help." Shale notices that her friends appear restive, glancing frequently in her direction.

"Tell me—how did you come to discover this cave?" Alexandre would like to better understand her work in order to represent it to Octavio as nonthreatening, as an advantage.

"I was following the work of Spanish archaeologist Jesús Carballo on Neolithic sites in the Sierra de Atapuerca. As you no doubt know, the mountain pass in that area is part of the pilgrim route to Santiago de Compostela and contains a causeway built by the Romans. As a result, I became interested in Roman roads and mining. Where there is mining, there are caves. Pliny the Elder wrote of the gold mines of Las Médulas and the copper mines of Rio Tinto. These are the most famous mines, but Galicia is rich in minerals and many prospectors have taken to your hills. An account of a cave-in located in the Serra de San Mamede caught my attention. The various mine shafts were named for figures found on the walls of a nearby cave. Essentially, prehistoric cave art."

"Still, such a small clue?"

"Yes and no. What I was reading was a letter, highly descriptive, and the writer kindly included a map of the area and the mine site. I believe he was corresponding with his business partner. Putting in an urgent request for supplies and manpower. It was an eureka letter, at least for me."

"And this letter has only come to light now?"

"The Ruta de la Plata led me to it."

"The Silver Route? How so?"

"Well, Pliny the Elder pointed me in the right direction. In AD 73 he wrote of a road he called the Vía de la Plata. As I'm sure you know, the Roman's built a nine hundred-kilometre causeway to transport precious metals mined in northern Spain south and presumably on to Rome. I was searching through the Smithsonian archives and came upon an eighteenth century atlas. Lifting the dusty book down from an overhead shelf, the spine gave a mighty groan, the covers opened like two stiff wings and the letter floated to the floor."

Alexandre recognizes Shale's rapt expression and revels in it. "The innumerable Roman roads are still followed," he says. "The Roman bridges still crossed. Take the Alcántara Bridge built of granite without mortar in AD 105."

"Yes, if we took it now, we could escape into Portugal." Her direct gaze shifts from Dr. Castro to her friends gathered behind him.

"Escape"— the word is born on Pat's breath.

Dr. Castro is startled. He turns to the women marshalled at his shoulder. "In due course. In the meantime, I have a lion to beard."

Silent confusion.

"El Comandante's second name is Leonidas."

"So, code name, 'El Comandante' is Octavio Leonidas Castro. And Dr. Castro, code name, 'The Brother' is?" Dorothy's manner makes it clear she wants a formal introduction that recognizes they are all players on this stage.

"Alexandre Sebastián Castro."

"Since you have our curriculum vitae in those little notebooks, we will dispense with any further introductions. However, I would like to make it perfectly clear that we are all in this together. At least, the Canadian contingent?" Dorothy says.

Alexandre smiles his charming smile while wondering if all Canadian women are so forthright? "Of course, while I retire to the lion's den, I'm sure Dr. Clifden will enlighten you." He leaves, taking the frisson with him.

"We have a plan." Shale leaves the desk and takes a seat on a sofa that faces the tall windows. The others follow suit, occupying overstuffed wing chairs with sagging springs and soiled upholstery.

The windows capture Shale's attention for a moment before she turns her gaze to the others. "I am truly sorry. This is my fault. I should never have brought you here."

"We're big girls. We knew the score.' Sheila grins at Shale. "Now tell us how you're going to get us out of here before I develop housemaid's knee."

"Yes." Dorothy adds, "I'm already suffering from what the devoted call 'nun's knee.' Although I'm enjoying reading the floor."

"Reading the floor?" Pat narrows her dark eyes.

"And writing the floor. Rat shit can be a poet's best friend—well, under these circumstances, at any rate."

Sheila looks from Dorothy to Shale. "Is she off her rocker? This place—"

Shale glances at the door before she speaks, "In the dungeon—a section of the floor between the wall and the stairs leading to the courtyard—we have made it our blackboard. Use the pointed corner of your scraping tool to incise messages in the filth."

Dorothy is also aware that time is short. "The plan?"

"To contact the Smithsonian—"

"Uncle Sam's going to rescue us?" Pat interjects.

"No, Uncle Sam isn't in the business of taking care of wayward citizens. He made that perfectly clear when the likes of Louis Fischer, a correspondent for *The Nation*, disappeared in Madrid."

"What then?"

"Money, we—"

୨ᦱ୨ᦱ

The door bursts open, the guards hustle them off to the dungeon and the rat shit floor.

Sheila has claimed the blackboard. Now she writes on the floor,

Can we trust The Brother?

There is a rhythm to the scrape, scrape of Shale's trowel. She is humming and remembering the four of them in the pub around the corner from Canada House in London. They are singing the popular Bing Crosby song, *Pennies from Heaven*. The other patrons cheer them on as they swill beer and belt out the refrain. An innocent time. So much has happened since then.

Pat sings softly. "Rain, Rain, Pennies, Pennies, Heaven, Heaven."

The others find their voices. The guards ignore them until Dr. Castro appears in the passage. The men stamp out their cigarettes on the stone stairs. The Brother directs the women up the steps to the courtyard. He stops at the top of the staircase, turns, and in a voice edged with steel, he says to the guards, "Clean up your mess, now."

To the women seated on the benches, Dr. Castro says with some wonder, "You were singing?"

"Reminiscing really." Shale looks to the others. "The evening we met for the first time—in London."

"You were in a recital?" He seems amused.

"We were in a pub. We met at Canada House—a lecture given by a young Canadian studying at Cambridge."

"*The Art of Code and The Code of Art*—an ambitious title reasonably rendered," Pat passes judgement.

"Yes, he managed to 'marshall' a rather diverse set of characters to support his thesis. From Pythagoras to Marcel Duchamp, no less," Sheila adds with a wry smile.

"No. Was it credible?"

"Fascinating, yes. Credible, beyond our telling," Dorothy answers his question. "We all took notes, but the best interpretation? Pat's page of doodles. Captured the essence."

Dr. Castro studies them closely. "So, you are here because of a chance meeting? You were strangers before?"

The women look at each other, almost as amazed as the good doctor.

"Kismet?" Dorothy muses.

"Destiny?" Pat believes in fate.

"No, just good, plain Canadian sang-froid. We're a nation of explorers." Sheila gives a curt nod. "High-minded enough never to leave a compeer in the lurch."

Silence.

Dr. Castro speaks with resolve. "For our plan to work, we will need all the cold-blooded composure and determination we can muster."

"You spoke with El Comandante?" Shale reconfirms.

"Yes, we spoke. Did he listen? Remains to be seen." Dr. Castro stares at his hands.

"This cold-blooded plan—" Dorothy looks from The Brother to Shale. "Time to tell the rest of us."

"I didn't have a chance to before we were hustled off to the dungeon," Shale explains.

"For now, I am taking things into my own hands." He turns to Shale. "We will call the Smithsonian within the hour. Will we find the Secretary there?"

"What day of the week is it?"

"Tuesday."

"And the time?"

The Brother checks his wristwatch. "It's 12:40. Will the Secretary be in his office?"

"Oh, yes. Given the time difference."

"What will you tell him?" The Brother tries for calm neutrality in face and voice."

"For the moment, I will tell Secretary Abbot that we are your guests."

The other women, assuming they are watched from beyond the colonnade, refrain from derisive laughter; sour smiles will do.

The Brother nods. "How long will it take him to make a decision?"

"Well, I will remind him that our time in Spain is limited, growing shorter by the minute. He is well aware of the militant situation here." Shale pauses. "Charles— Secretary Abbot—will most certainly ask about my fieldwork. He will make a decision more quickly if my work is nearing completion and our departure from Spain is imminent."

"In that case, I will beard the Leonidas one more time. Then we will call Washington. In the meantime, the best place for you ladies is the gallery. And, Dr. Clifden, if you would draw up a list of artifacts that might interest The Secretary, we could have it to hand when we make our overseas call."

Before Alexandre leaves them in the gallery, he reminds Shale that they must be cautious. "Know that you are being watched. My brother's priest spies for him. And, yes, he does understand the English language."

"What if someone asks what I'm doing?"

"I've instructed you to compile an inventory. That's all they need to know."

Once Alexandre has left, Shale takes the women to the display case farthest from the door. "This case holds a Bronze Age flesh-hook." Her voice takes on the tone and pitch of a lecture. "A metal shaft with sharp hooks or barbs like the one we see here was attached to a long wooden handle. What do you think it was used for?"

While the women speculate, she says in a quiet voice, "Keep talking while I tell you about the plan."

Under an increasingly outrageous discussion that has veered off into descriptions of torture, Shale outlines what it will take to get them out of Spain in no more than three weeks.

♋♋♋

On her knees, Pat studies the rat shit blackboard. Messages, yes, but no poetry. She gets to work with her makeshift stylus, the letters are small and fine:

Let us stand together, till the cool evening settles this silent place and having seen the hatted priest move in the still shadow—

But the shadow isn't still; it hovers over her, grabbing her roughly by the arm. She raises the scraper to draw the guard's eyes away from the floor. He knocks it from her hand and looks into her face to discern her intent.

The guard is pushing her through a door in the courtyard. She is startled to find herself on the street, being dragged toward a farm truck. He lifts her like a child into the open box of the truck. The others are there, sitting on the straw-covered boards of the flatbed. There are knapsacks and goatskin bags of water, she suspects, but is hoping for wine. Pat looks from one to the other of her friends. They remain silent. The guard close by.

Dr. Castro arrives in a rush and orders the guard into the passenger's seat. They watch as The Brother swings into the cab and takes the steering wheel. They are gone without a word.

The wind flies in their faces, stealing their words. They huddle together. Leaving the cobbled street and its rough ride, they pull up their bandanas and close their eyes against the red dust.

Hours whistle down the wind. Towns, then villages fall behind. Shale recognizes the cry of the Eurasian sparrow hawk. Lifting her dirt-red eyes to the sky, a common buzzard comes into view. The truck engine labours, and Shale realizes they are climbing beyond scrub into a forest that hides the rare Montederramo birches. Soon, they will be hefting the knapsacks onto their backs: almost a relief; certainly a joy. They will not reach the cave until tomorrow.

3

S. H. E. CAVE

Serra de San Mamede, Galicia

3

S.H.E. CAVE

The trail is rocky underfoot. Surrounded by scrub bush, the ascent is steep. Gradually they leave the umbra lands and are embraced by fern-green banks and moss-hung trees. There is cooling shade among the birches. Single file, they fall into a rhythmic silence deepened by the tree tapping of a great spotted woodpecker.

As they climb higher, Shale anticipates the sharp cries of kestrels and snake eagles. She looks back at her companions. The women seem at home here in the Serra de San Mamede, ironically, more so than Dr. Castro.

A few more hours and they will stop for the night, taking shelter in a stone hut with slate roof and sod-covered porch. A resting place for shepherds, she assumes. Shepherds, indeed . . . is this her flock following behind? And is there a wolf in sheep's clothing among them? Shale has not answered this question to her satisfaction. Is self-interest outweighing familial duty for Dr. Castro? If so, will it remain the driving force long enough to see them out of Spain? If she can instill a sense of awe in him, an understanding of the magnitude of her discovery and its impact on the story of our kind, will it keep him steadfast? A humanist, a man of science . . . surely, he has vision? All these questions . . . only time will tell, but how much time? Their time is running out.

$$\infty\infty\infty$$

The hut is cramped, but at least there is a table to set out their humble meal: bread, cheese, and sausage washed down with water tasting faintly of wine. They've spread the blankets from their knapsacks on the hard-packed earth floor.

"How long has El Comandante given us?" Shale asks The Brother.

"There is enough food and water if we are frugal for five days maybe six," Alexandre replies from his place by the door.

"Then what?" Sheila asks.

"Then we return to the road, where the truck will be waiting with provisions."

"All of us?" Shale is now just a voice in the darkness.

"Yes, it will require all of us to pack the food and water back up the mountain.

It is quiet enough to hear the night creatures.

"The guards could be your pack animals, you know. If you would allow it, Dr. Clifden."

"No, absolutely not. The location of the cave remains with us. No one else."

Pat, in her best conciliatory voice, asks The Brother if he had roamed these mountains as a youth?

"No, we didn't venture this far from home. Our days were taken up with tutors of one sort or another."

"You didn't attend school?"

"School came to us. Along with equestrian and arms masters."

"Ah, I wish school had come to me." Pat is wistful.

"What! You didn't care for St. Hilda's?" Shale taunts. She and Pat had discovered that they both had attended St. Hilda's Girls School in Calgary.

"At first, yes. But I would have much preferred fencing lessons and horse riding. I learned to ride Indian ponies on the prairies— bareback with only a piece of rope for a bridle."

"Not part of the curriculum when I attended St. Hilda's." Shale sounds crestfallen.

"No. I spent my summers at the Sarcee Camp." Pat remembers she has revealed this information to Shale only. "You see, my father was with the Lord Strathcona's Horse, and they held manoeuvres with other army regiments near the Sarcee Reserve, south of

Calgary." For The Brother's benefit, she adds, "The town of Calgary is in Western Canada—land of mountains, rivers and of course, mixed grass prairies. Home to Native peoples for millennia."

"Miss Page, your childhood was an adventure, while mine was a servitude." Alexandre seems moved. "Please tell us more."

"All right . . . I rode a cayuse called Zena—"

"A what?" Dorothy interjects.

"Oh, a wild horse tamed by the Natives, the Sarcee. One ride I'll never forget as long as I live—my father and I galloped out across the brown hills toward the endless blue sky. I spotted a small box on the open prairie. As we got closer, we could see what had spilled out. A skeleton—a baby wrapped in a brightly beaded belt and wearing bead bracelets, all of it holding bleached bones together."

The darkness holds them separate, alone with those fragile bones.

Sheila dispels the silence. "I have a horse named Fiddle. I learned to ride and hunt while teaching school at Dog Creek—gold rush country in Northern British Columbia."

"Another adventuress." Alexandre is amused and fascinated by these Canadians.

"More like a teacher trying to find work during hard times. The only offer I had—one room schoolhouse, nine students of varying ages in the tawny Cariboo Mountains."

"Horses," Shale muses, "ever present. There in prehistory, gracing the walls."

"What of flesh-and-blood horses, Dr. Clifden?" The voice comes from the direction of the hut door.

"Ah, more leading than riding, Dr. Castro. My early experiences included leading packhorses laden with fossils down mountain trails, sometimes riding them back up to the quarry."

"Is it typical for Canadian children to be given such independence?" Alexandre seems pensive.

"It is when your mother has died." Shale creates a ripple in the darkness.

"Or your father." Sheila amplifies it.

"In my experience, even with two parents, Canadian children grow up quickly. You must understand, we are a young nation, still carving out a place in rock and soil." Dorothy pauses. "My parents treated my sister and me as if we were adults, even when we were very young."

"Rock and soil. What sort of things were expected of you, may I ask?" Alexandre has become Dr. Castro, psychologist.

"Oh, well." Dorothy feels she might have been too forthcoming. "At the dinner table we discussed politics, religion, literature. My father expected us to have opinions—well-informed ideas based on the books he assigned us to read."

"My goodness, you were seen and heard. How very un-British." Sheila's voice is recognizable in the darkness by its slight note of sadness. "Where were your parents from?"

"They were Britannia's wayward children, journalists for the *Winnipeg Telegram*." Surprisingly, Dorothy sounds shy. "Winnipeg, where they met, married and I was born—rooted in the prairie soil."

"Of course you write?" Pat is hopeful, a fellow scribbler.

"In the blood. My mother took to poetry like Victorian ladies took to the fainting couch. She saw to it that I published by the time I was nineteen. And at the end of my second year of university, my father got me a job as a reporter for the *Winnipeg Tribune*."

"Mother as muse, my mother and I made books when I was a toddler." The dark encourages Pat to reminisce. "My parents read me nursery rhymes, I drew pictures, and then we fashioned them into books made of rag paper. Rose, my mother, is a very creative soul. And stunningly beautiful." A soft laugh changes the air. "Should daughters say such things?" The laugh again.

"Heavens, you two are accomplished." Sheila is sincere. "With the exception of a few individually published poems, my literary efforts are all in the academic realm."

"Accomplished," Pat snorts. "A children's book with the title *Wisdom from Nonsense Land* hardly qualifies. Although it was very good." Dark minutes pass. "Mind you, I did have a poem published in the *London Observer*. And I have written for radio, but that's small potatoes."

"Dr. Clifden, it appears you have chosen admirable companions—all in the course of one evening in a London pub. You are a fine judge of character, it seems." Alexandre has not had much experience with the aspirations of women.

"I'm sure the beer, then the whiskey might have had something to do with it." The wind has slid down the mountain to rattle the flimsy porch, and capture their attention. "To be fair, we all share a sense of urgency. The world is preparing to destruct."

"It's just the wind in the roof," Pat points out, causing them to laugh.

"Out of desperation is born destruction." Dorothy is thinking of Nick Zynchuk's funeral in Montreal, where people lined the streets chanting "Bread not lead." Nick . . . an immigrant worker shot by police while being evicted from his boardinghouse for not paying the rent.

"These have been desperate years, no doubt," Sheila commiserates. "God flung me down in Dog Creek, or so I thought, but living on the edge of the world—the most northern point of the Mojave Desert, where camels had been used to build the railroad—I found peace." Sheila takes a big breath.

"Were you accepted?" Dr. Castro asks. "In this remote place, a frontier town?" What a fascinating study subject she would make.

"It would seem so. I was gifted the heart of a butchered steer." Even in the dark, Sheila has divined the reason for his interest.

There is a gasp within the stone walls, then laughter.

"We must seem like alien creatures to you, Dr. Castro." There is a mocking note in Pat's voice. "Is it because we are Canadians or because we are women?"

There is more wind than breath in the rude hut.

"As professional women, I'm sure you understand how consuming a chosen field can be. So, hopefully, you will forgive my questions. And no, you are not alien; you're intriguing."

"Ah, yes, 'intrigue.' There's the watchword for our little party of professionals." Dorothy is not inclined to trust The Brother's motives in this venture. She senses something veiled.

Shale recognizes Dorothy's reservations. Nevertheless, it's all they've got; he's all they've got. Watch and see, she thinks, before suggesting they bank some sleep against tomorrow's climb. It only gets steeper—the mountain, the stakes. Once she leads Dr. Castro to the cave, she has lost control; essentially her discovery is open to the world. A world of one at the moment, but one is enough. Oh, yes, the women know, but they have no claim—The Brother does.

The party is back on the trail just after dawn and a scant breakfast. They walk, no breath for talk, and stop briefly to run hands over the papery bark of the unique Montederramo birches.

By mid-afternoon they have reached a rocky outcrop just below the summit. Here, they find the abandoned mine, the entrance barely visible, hidden by green and yellow scrub. They have left behind the oaks, mountain ash, and ferns, while the Spanish broom, golden and fragrant, has followed them to higher ground. They will make camp at the mine, using the entrance for shelter. Piled inside are the remains of wooden boxes that on previous visits they had scavenged from the mine site and, using Shale's hatchet, reduced to firewood. The hatchet hidden, but handy.

Shale comes out of the mine with a bundle of what looks like dry grass in her arms. She throws it on a waste pile while asking to borrow Alexandre's knife. "To cut more bedding," she says. "The broom shoots are like rushes: they make good ground cover."

"I'll do it. How much do we need?"

She takes his meaning. "Enough to cover the shaft floor at the entrance. This is our camp."

"I'll lay a fire, shall I?" Sheila asks.

"Yes, thanks." The women share a meaningful look. The hatchet goes unmentioned. "When we're done setting up camp, we'll go around to the SHE Cave."

Alexandre turns to Shale, the broom in his hands, the yellow flowers a bouquet. "She cave?"

"Yes, S-H-E—Smithsonian Historical Expedition." Shale is precise.

"But we like to call it, 'Shale's Historical Enigma'." Pat mimics Shale's formal tone.

"An 'enigma,' I see." He looks from one to the other for enlightenment. "Enigma—a mystery, a riddle, a secret?"

"Perhaps a conundrum, which is what we find ourselves in," Dorothy suggests. "How do you think this will end, Dr. Castro?"

"I'm no oracle," Miss Livesay. "Especially not in these times. But take heart, I can be conniving."

"Small comfort," Sheila whispers from behind an armload

of kindling.

Shale suspects The Brother knows El Comandante all too well. Most certainly he has a backup plan in the event El Comandante considers them more valuable than money.

♋♋♋

They climb the slope. There is no beaten path. This is purposeful on Shale's part. She leads them by a different route each time they access the cave, minimizing the signs of their presence.

Next, they must circumvent a promontory, the sheer cliffs above their heads. More than once birds have commented on this intrusion, their droppings the colour of writing paper.

Shale halts, waiting for them to catch up. The troop arrives. Shale stares at Alexandre.

He looks around in confusion. "Are we taking a break? We need one—the pace you set," he says to Shale.

"What do you see, Dr. Castro?"

"More of the same. Why do you ask?"

"We are at the cave," Pat volunteers.

While he catches his breath, Alexandre studies his surroundings.

"The reason the cave has remained undiscovered, at least before and after the miners, is that the entrance is an overlapping crack in the cliff wall, hidden by brush." Shale refrains from pointing out its hiding place. Curious to see how someone might locate it. "The miners found it by accident, of course. Perhaps while searching for game or firewood. Or doing some additional prospecting."

Impatient with this hide-and-seek, Dorothy pushes the brush aside and disappears before Alexandre's eyes. He is standing in front of the entrance.

The women slip through one by one. Alexandre is not so lucky. It is a tight squeeze for him. He is too tall, but cannot duck down because he is so tightly wedged between the walls. He must retreat and try a different tactic. He inserts himself head first, at an angle, his hands splayed against the rock wall to hold him upright while his legs trail his body. Finally, he emerges, red-faced.

"A difficult birth for you," Shale remarks, her voice echoes as if mocking.

Sheila strikes a match and lights a kerosene lantern. Their shadows crowd the walls. They are in a passage that is arched and round-sided. Sheila leads the way. Within half-a-dozen metres the passage narrows, then opens magnanimously into a cavern.

Sheila veers off to the right, taking light with her. The others stubble behind, only to be stopped in their tracks by a stampede of horses thundering across a wall.

Alexandre is startled, by their beauty, yes, but more by their prescience: his thoughts manifest on the wall.

"The Horse Gallery," Pat announces with a flourish. "My favourite drawings, my favourite place to draw."

"Wild beauty. Beyond words. Trying to describe these creatures takes every ounce of my skill as a writer," Dorothy adds.

Shale is pleased by Alexandre's reaction. He seems entranced. It is what she had hoped for: a strong basis for his commitment. She will indoctrinate him with words, but strong actions require strong feelings. For now, she'll let him take it in, bolstered by the sense of reverence her friends bring to this special place.

To keep the moment from faltering, Shale signals Sheila to take the light and their shadows to the opposite gallery. Here, bison look on as reindeer stags clash. Fantastical is the intricacy of their antlers climbing the wall to the ceiling. A tracery fine and powerful. An image unto itself.

Again, the rapt expression is there on Alexandre's face. Shale is heartened. Her cave just may give birth to a new acolyte.

Once back in the central area of the cavern, Sheila holds the lantern high, casting light on the ceiling. A phalanx of stalactites threatens them from above. Rough rock spears bristle from the ceiling, having pierced enormous bears many times over. Engraved with deep, robust lines accentuated with charcoal, the bears seem oblivious to their condition. In fact, they appear to be smiling at the watchers, a knowing smile that makes it clear humans are more vulnerable than cave bears.

Sheila moves toward the top end of the cavern, the wall of which curves away to the left and right.

Once there, an opening reveals narrow passages leading to more mystery.

The lantern sputters, and Shale halts the party. "The kerosene is low in the lamp; we should make our way out. Tomorrow is another day."

☙ ❧ ☙ ❧

The campfire isn't enough to dim the stars, even though the SHE party huddles close to the flames. The nights are cold in the mountains.

In response to Alexandre's many questions, Shale has resorted to outlining the history of prehistoric research. She gets no further than 1895 and the declaration by German Professor Leo Frobenius that this year was a turning point, the birth of a "modern conception of the early periods of human culture." And what was the impetus? A cave found in Northern Spain some sixteen years earlier by Baron Sautuola. The ice age paintings of the Altamira Cave were in Frobenius's estimation "neither primitive nor simple." He even went so far as to say, "These pictures were true and great works of art." This did not reflect the thinking of the time.

The modern conception of early human culture was to come from Leo Frobenius. Only after he declared the current science and its scientists "lazy, phlegmatic, and stupid." He proposed that a "science of culture," a true "culture-morphology" would require dedicated research institutions and expeditions. Shale finishes by saying, "So, you see, my profession is, to all intents and purposes, only forty years old."

All the while Alexandre is nodding his head in acknowledgement. "Not unlike my own profession. A Russian not a German set the course."

A look of surprise crosses Dorothy's face. "How so? What of Herr Freud?"

"Or for that matter, René Descartes?" Sheila joins the inquiry.

"I am speaking of Ivan Pavlov and the Science of Behaviour. The breakthrough came with Pavlov's discovery of Conditioned Reflexes, moving psychology beyond philosophy and introspection. It's not enough to describe and explain the psyche, our goal should be to predict and control— a 'modern conception' I became acquainted with at Harvard."

"How modern?" Shale asks.

"Ivan Petrovich Pavlov introduced his idea in 1904, during his Nobel Prize acceptance speech."

Dorothy is restive, poking at the fire with a stick and sending sparks into the night sky.

"I could teach you how to send smoke signals," Pat says to Dorothy.

"You are an impertinent imp" is Dorothy's response.

"Horsefeathers. We could signal Shale's boss in Washington. Get him to send the navy."

"Dr. Abbot has already been alerted," Shale says quietly.

They look at her wordless.

"The call I made before we left to come here."

"I don't understand," Alexandre says across the fire. "I was in the room. I heard your conversation."

"You heard me tell Dr. Abbot that 'no, the Castro Collection does not contain Sabine artifacts, not even a fibula from a woman's cloak'."

"That is true. There are no fibulae in my grandfather's collection." Alexandre is even more perplexed.

"You see, Dr. Abbot had not asked a question, but he most certainly would have understood the reference to the Sabine women."

"And what would he have understood?"

"Abduction. The Romans abducted Sabine women to populate the newly founded Rome."

"What will he do?" Sheila asks.

"For now, he'll inform the appropriate government agencies. Then it's a waiting game. We should look to our own futures. We'll begin tomorrow morning at dawn. The sooner we document the cave, the sooner we can—"

"Yes?"

"Do whatever it takes to get home."

༄༅༄༅

The women have picked up where they left off weeks ago. They have changed into their field clothes. A relief, the clothes they had left in the cave are cleaner by far than the ones they were wearing. They have retrieved their journals, pens, and coloured pencils from various hiding places in the cave and are at work with barely a word between them.

Alexandre stands in the cavern, trying to imagine the life here thousands of years ago. How is it those people, those artists, have vanished so completely, yet their creations live on? An irony that can never be reconciled: objects are immutable; humans are not. Is that what makes artifacts so valuable to us? The connection so strong, that these women willingly risked their lives to preserve what connects us to ourselves? It is no wonder that Octavio does not believe them. He is of the here and now, and has never been interested in what came before. Not even when their grandfather tried to pique their childish curiosity.

Shale appears at Alexandre's side, notebook in hand. "I would like you to be our cartographer. Unfortunately, I have no tools for measuring, so we will resort to pacing. If you pace along the walls, draw a diagram and note the number of paces, eventually we should have a map of the cavern and its two passages."

"Of course, consider it done."

"Start at the opening where we enter the cliff. Draw the orifice as overlapping." Shale leaves him to it and crosses to the head of the cavern, disappearing down the left passage.

As he watches her go, it occurs to him that he has not explored those upper passages. Well, he'll pace them off soon enough.

As Alexandre maps the cavern, it becomes apparent that the women work according to invisible boundaries. The cavern, ostensibly an ovoid, seems to be sectioned in to four equal parts.

The space is profoundly quiet, except for him scraping and stumbling along the rough floor and wall. He wonders what kind of results this form of subjective documentation will yield. Cameras would be useful tools in this work. He supposes that a proper expedition would be equipped with more than paper and pencils. It must be rather galling for Dr. Clifden. Probably not up to her scientific standards.

There is so much to record, big and small. When he is finished with his map, perhaps he can have a closer look, maybe even get a peek inside the SHE notebooks.

He reaches the head of the cavern, having mapped the left wall. Rather than complete the ovoid, Alexandre decides to continue pacing along the left passage. As he draws the passage wall and records the paces, he realizes the passage is gradually curving upward. For some unknown reason he had expected it to be straight, like the hall that led to his office at the university. But, no, the gradual arc has become a bend where the floor begins to slope downward. Ahead, there is a glow. The passage leads to a small cave. Inside the entrance, pillars as smooth as tusks rise from floor to ceiling. He pauses to add this strange cavity to his map. Dr. Clifden's sanctuary.

When he looks up from the page, Dr. Clifden is standing in front of him, blocking his view and the light from her lantern. Over her shoulder, he sees a strange configuration. Where her shadow has muted the stark reflection of the white walls, there are standing figures. It is as if she has ghosts at her back.

Shale has seen the recognition in his eyes. She picks up his lantern from the floor and moves forward, forcing him out of the entrance and into the passage.

"There are figures—human figures, life-size." Alexandre is still staring over her shoulder.

"A semblance of human figures."

"What does it mean?"

"I can't be sure."

"So, they could be recent?"

"Recent is relative. Anything is possible at this stage. This gallery must be assessed as a whole. There are familiar and unfamiliar elements."

"May I see?" Alexandre is intrigued.

"When I have finished my documentation, yes. Until then, the grotto must remain free of contamination. As free as possible."

"Of, course. Perhaps we could discuss your findings this evening?"

"Perhaps."

Shale watches him pace the opposite wall on his way out. She raises her hand as if to halt him. "Dr. Castro, there is also a small cave at the end of the right passage. Please refrain from entering it."

♋♋♋

Sheila stirs the pot as a discussion about the state of the world increases in volume. She stops listening to the words, hearing only the sound of her comrades' voices echoing off the mountain—a sound that raises the hairs on her arms. Fear, her body is registering fear.

She turns, holds up the stir-stick, and declares, "The world is mad, bad, and sad. Don't let it poison our sanctuary here."

Startled into silence, they study the dripping stick as if it were a mace, giving the holder the right to speak.

"Supper ready?" Dorothy asks, being the mother of necessity.

"Yes," Sheila says, "I would gladly listen to the sounds of slurping and slobbering."

They laugh and hold out their bowls. Sheila dips a cup into the mess of salt pork, beans, onion, and fills their bowls.

"So, Sheila, what do you consider proper dinner conversation? And don't say religion." Dorothy hides her grin behind her spoon.

"Well, yes, I was going to speak of religion." Sheila turns to Shale. "Was our cave a place of worship?"

"In as much as we worship those things that are intrinsic to our lives."

"The animals for instance," Pat points out.

"Yes,"—Shale pauses—"but I believe not just the animals, but the act of rendering them on the walls."

"Art. They worshipped art?" Alexandre appears surprised.

Shale redirects his question. "The act of creation. It is more to us mere mortals than simply procreation."

"Art for art's sake," Dorothy offers.

"Art for the sake of the moment, not for the sake of posterity. This is an act of enrichment for the artist and the viewer."

"If I understand your premise: art fulfills a deep need"—Alexandre hesitates—"perhaps as intrinsic to humans as food and water."

"We are more than flesh and blood—"

"For better or for worse," Pat amends Shale's dictum.

"What has led you to this theory, Dr. Clifden?" Alexandre would like something more empirical.

"Technique. What the artist sees in the rock."

"I don't understand?"

"Dr. Castro, are you familiar with Hermann Rorschach?"

"The Dr. Rorschach, the Swiss psychiatrist?" Sheila speaks as if of a friend.

"Yes," Shale answers with a note of surprise in her voice.

"My father corresponded with Klecks."

"With whom?" It is Alexandre's turn for bewilderment.

"Inkblot. That was Dr. Rorschach's nickname from childhood, when klecksography first fascinated him. You know, making pictures out of inkblots." Sheila looks from Shale to Alexandre. "At home, in my father's house, our priest was teaching me German and I acted as my father's translator. He was interested in using Dr. Rorschach's inkblots as an analytical tool. My father was hoping this technique would be a point of entry with his patients at the asylum."

Inkblots?" Pat is shaking her head.

Sheila dips the cup into the stew pot and retrieves a small amount of liquid. She levels a patch of soil with her foot and pours the gravy from the cup onto the ground all at once. It splashes, raising dust that falls back to earth as droplets. "Come here, Pat. Take my place on the log. Now, stare into the stain at your feet and tell us what you see."

"That's easy. I see our supper going to waste on the ground."

"Don't be such a literalist. Look into the stain the way Leonardo da Vinci would have."

"What?"

"I'll enlighten you, only after you tell me what your inner eye, your artist's eye sees."

"Well, if you put it that way . . . let me see . . . . A spider gathering up her countless offspring." Pat looks up at Sheila. "Your turn."

"The great Leonardo da Vinci once advised painters to look carefully at stains on walls or at walls made of different kinds of stone, telling them they would see landscapes, figures with strange expressions, or outlandish costumes. In other words, it's all in the eye and the imagination of the beholder."

Alexandre claps. "Well done, Miss Doherty. A fine lesson." He turns to Shale. "You were saying?"

"My colleagues and I have observed that prehistoric painters, engravers, and sculptures took advantage of nature. A bulge in a rock wall becomes a bison's hump, a curving crack the neck of a horse, a rock projection takes on human characteristics. This relationship between artist and rock is obvious to the viewer. I am exploring a less obvious relationship."

"And Rorschach?" Alexandre reminds her.

"Da Vinci" is Shale's reply. "Stains on walls, different kinds of stone. The primitives were skilled at seeing with the inner eye. We have been looking at prehistoric art with our eyes not theirs. We must learn to see the way they did."

"And what of the grottos in the SHE Cave?" Alexandre has not forgotten Shale's earlier promise.

"Proof" is her answer.

"Of your theory?" Alexandre wants her to be definitive.

"I believe so. And Sheila's experiment with Pat confirms that the inner eye is a human trait."

"What have you found?" Intrigued, Alexandre is relentless.

"Projecting rock figures, as you observed. Engraved skull bones. And paintings that are not animals." Shale, looking for a diversion, stands with the intent of taking the stew pot off the fire.

"If they're not animals, what are they?" Sheila is the first to ask, as she helps Shale put a cover on the pot and weigh it down with a large stone.

"Let's just say for now—the grottos present a new visual language."

"But—"

"That is as much as I will say. Now to bed. We start at first light. Our time here is short."

With stone in place, Shale and Sheila each take a handle and carry the pot toward the mouth of the mine shaft. Alexandre is ahead of them and stops to move a wooden door made of rough planks that appears to be leaning against the rock face. His actions reveal a deep hidey-hole cut into the native rock. There are mining tools stored inside, as well as the SHE supplies. The women cache the cooking pot in this makeshift storage cupboard. There is enough supper left over to provide them with breakfast. Alexandre lifts the heavy door back into place, then drags a tree stump over to hold the door closed.

Once in the tunnel entrance, they unroll their blankets across the broom shoots covering the dirt floor. The shifting and settling stops long enough for the dark to descend on them.

Out of the silence comes Alexandre's voice, "Dr. Clifden . . . you called these prehistoric peoples 'the primitives.' Would you define 'primitive' for me?"

"That sounds like a simple request, but is far from it. I will say that my definition is diametrically opposed to nineteenth-century thinking. To the idea that evolution is progressive—from inferior to superior. And superior is how the nineteenth century defined itself. That art evolves is a judgement. That art is an human impulse is a truth."

"Surely, you would agree that primitive art is simplistic?"

"Compared to what?"

"The Sistine Chapel." Alex avails himself of the Renaissance for his proof.

There are gasps in the dark.

"Art is of its time and place. The ceiling of the SHE Cave could in fact be the Sistine Chapel of its culture. Prehistoric peoples were highly innovative in every aspect of their lives. Their survival—our survival depended upon it."

"Our materialistic culture does not necessarily make us superior." Dorothy joins the discussion. "I have seen inside factories, inside tenements—I see nothing superior in slave labour and starving children."

"Stimmung," Alex whispers into the rock-solid dark.

There is complete silence—this foreign word coming on the heels of Dorothy's pronouncement.

With bewilderment in her voice, Sheila utters, "'Mood'? Or do you mean 'atmosphere'? And why?"

"My apologies," Alex says. "I was considering the idea of art as a human impulse. Then I remembered a discussion I had with a Harvard friend. We talked of Wassily Kandinsky and his interpretation of the German 'Stimmung' as 'essential spirit.'"

"The Russian artist, right?" Pat asks. "Who wrote a book called, *Concerning the Spiritual in Art.*"

"Yes, one and the same. At the time, my friend, Robert Goldwater, was completing his MA in art history."

"Kandinsky writes of internal truths expressed in art, as does the German ethnologist and archaeologist, Leo Frobenius," Shale adds. "It is because of Professor Frobenius that I highly value your work, my friends."

"Tell us more," Sheila demands.

"A few words from the great man himself should suffice. About the use of cameras to document prehistoric cave art, Professor Frobenius states, 'A lens cannot differentiate between that which is essential and that which is not. So, there is nothing left but to have the pictures copied by hand, something which is not easy and which can be done satisfactorily only by those who have immersed themselves in the material and are sensitive to the spirit and mentality of an age which has passed.'"

There is an unladylike snort from Pat. "You memorized that word for word?"

"Yes." Shale is not fazed. "It is an integral part of my address to each new field team I lead. If you must know."

"Oh, well, I'm glad you consider us a worthy field team." Even in the dark it is apparent Dorothy's sentiment is genuine.

The others join in: "Hear, hear."

ꙮꙮꙮ

Entering the SHE Cave single file, they are all lined up behind Shale like votaries. As is her want, she stops for a moment before entering the "Great Room." The others suspect it is an act of devotion meant to open the way into this other world.

Moving forward, they all go to their work stations. Shale moves across the cave floor toward the far wall and the grottos. Before she can enter the passage, Pat stops her. "What you said last night about being sensitive to this art—how do I know if I'm sensitive? If I'm capturing the spirit? I don't know. Now I feel unsure of what I've done, of my sketches. What if they're not good enough?" Pat is on the verge of tears.

"Your eye is true, Pat. It's free, not jaded by the speculation that often confounds my profession. You are like a young Dorothy Garrod."

"Who?" more a chant than a question delivered in unison, the others having listened with rapt attention to Pat's confession.

"The scientist who put to rest the centuries-old idea that artifacts were otherworldly—that is, produced by thunder, flood, or angels."

In response to the clamour of disbelief, Shale holds up her hand for silence and continues, "Stone tools revealed by farmers' plows were thought to be the result of thunder and lightning breaking apart rocks. Ancient pottery—the result of muddy water solidifying in holes and animal burrows. As for angel craft— well, anything carved, such as bone, ivory, or polished stones, was attributed to heavenly bodies."

"No. Surely, this Dorothy is from the long-dead past." But then ten years ago is ancient history to young Pat.

"Not so long and not so dead. Dorothy Garrod's classic book on human origins was published in 1926. And she recently completed a dig at Mount Carmel that has uncovered important human fossils from the Stone Age."

"So, how would she view the SHE Cave—see the areas of rock and paint I sketch?"

"What has set Dorothy Garrod apart? You might well ask. She is not afraid to think for herself. Her book was a huge research project. But she is meticulous and managed to put all the pieces together to form a revolutionary picture of human advancement."

"So, you're saying that this Dorothy would expect me to see and think for myself?"

"As do I." Shale turns to enter the opening that leads to the grottos. "Now to work."

Trailing her hand along the rough rock wall of the passage,

she reflects on how good it felt to speak of her friend Dorothy Garrod. It has been some time since they had enjoyed each other's company. The war in Spain had meant that Shale had had no time to see Dorothy while passing through England on her way to Galicia. What, indeed, would Dorothy make of the SHE Cave, especially the grottos?

Shale has no sooner settled into the grotto to the left of the entrance, when she hears steps along the passage. Thinking it is Pat with more doubts, Shale speaks loud enough to be heard outside her small chamber. "Unless you're bringing me the engraved incisor of a giant cave bear, leave me to my work."

"And what work is that, exactly?"

The echo created by the walls of the passage cannot hide the fact that it is Dr. Castro interrupting her analysis of a section of stained wall at eye level.

"So, show me the tooth," she says over her shoulder.

"That's just a myth, you know. The Cave Bear Cult," he replies from outside her domain.

"I know, but how do you know?"

"As a boy, I was interested in such things. So my grandfather introduced me to Ursus spelaeus in the form of a box full of bones. He and I reconstructed the skeleton. Our cave bear still occupies the attic."

"You had an unusual upbringing."

"No more so than yours, I suspect. I had my grandfather's Collection, and you had the Smithsonian's." Alexandre steps into the grotto, to examine it more closely. "And what sort of cult do you have here, Dr. Clifton?"

Shale is not pleased by the intrusion. "Cult is a specious term, not used by my profession."

"Surely, there is meaning in these walls?" is his rejoinder.

"So we would like to believe, since they were wrought by human hands. Perhaps it was simply a pastime."

"Then why give it your undivided attention? This visual language."

"Ah, you were paying attention." Shale finally turns to look at him. "Can I assume you follow the thinking of Dr. Joseph Maes?"

Alexandre is caught off guard. He had been prepared for a

teacherly lesson in rendering art; instead, Shale has invoked his world. "Are we speaking of *La Psychologie de l'Art Négre?*"

"'To penetrate all its beauty and all its life,' we must understand the psychology of art."

"And what does the grotto artist tell you? What is he saying?"

"She has much to share—about death and birth."

"She?"

"The visual language of the grottos exhibit the female principle of symbiosis, while the style is imaginative and abstract."

"Is this more of your Professor Frobenius?"

"Frobenius, certainly, but there are a whole host of men making claims about primitive art. And we're short of time." She turns back to the grotto.

"Why do those human figures at the entrance not have mouths?" Alexandre is more curious than ever.

"They are silent. Silenced by death. No mouth means death."

"How do you know?"

"I've seen it before— at burial sites, ancient and modern. Now, if you please—"

"But what of your theory? The technique used to make the visual language, the art?"

Shale takes a deep breath, exacerbation setting in. She leaves the grotto. Reaching into the pocket of her jacket, she pulls out a fat piece of chalk. Normally used for writing route directions on cave walls, she lays it flat on its side and shades a portion of rock near at hand in the passage. Having laid down white dust in minute cracks, crevices and the pockmarked face of the stone, Shale turns to Alexandre. "What do you see?"

Confounded, Alexandre looks from her to the passage wall and back again.

"No, stare at the shaded patch on the wall. Take some of our valuable time, and look deeply. Then tell me what you see."

"After a time, Alexandre says, "A small boat surrounded by people."

"Is that image meaningful to you?"

"No, it's just what I see."

"Can you give it meaning? Is it symbolic?"

"Freedom. The ocean has always meant freedom to me."

Shale leaves Alexandre staring at the wall and disappears into the grotto and her work.

⁓⁓⁓

"One more day and we hit the trail," Shale announces over a stew made from the last of their provisions. "It's going to be a hungry march."

"That's just fine. I've had enough of this so-called 'food' anyway." Pat is looking gaunt. A tall, slim young woman to begin with, starvation does not look good on her.

Shale takes in the faces around the campfire. What she sees worries her. Her friends are the worst for wear. She must talk to Dr. Castro tonight. In the meantime, perhaps she can take their minds off their grumbling guts by giving them new tasks for the next day. "You have all documented as much as you can; now it's time for a treasure hunt. Tomorrow, we play in the dirt. We're going to scratch the surface and see if there are artifacts to be had."

"What of the grottos? Will we dig there?" Dorothy looks hopeful.

Shale understands why. She has yet to share the secrets of those chambers. "You might ask Dr. Castro what he learned about the grottos today."

The look Alexandre gives Shale implies 'well-played'. "I discovered that female artists are mutually beneficial abstract thinkers."

Sheila turns to Shale. "What is he blithering about?"

"Perhaps it is time I introduced you to the grottos. Yes, I've been keeping them to myself. For good reason. These sites and my analysis of them must be free of outside influences. That said, I believe I have come to understand the impulse behind these chambers."

"So, they belong to women? Is that what the good doctor is trying to say?" Dorothy looks pointedly at Alexandre. She's unhappy that he breached the sanctuaries before the rest of them.

"Let me introduce you to the ideas of Wilhelm Worringer and, more importantly, Herbert Kühn."

"Germans, I take it? Germans with ideas about women. We should be reminded of the example Friedrich Nietzsche set, before we take the words of Teutonic men too seriously." Dorothy's tone has a wider implication.

"What? You don't see yourself as a slave, a cow, a cat, even a bird? As for a friend, you cannot be that because you are not really human." Sheila stokes the campfire with a stick as she echoes Nietzsche's *Thus Spake Zarathustra.*

"Kühn views primitive art from the position of economics."

"How so?" Alexandre speaks first.

"For Kühn, there are two different forms in primitive art. One he calls sensory or naturalistic and the other imaginative or abstract. Sensory art imitates the outside world, while imaginative art expresses the inner world, the mind and spirit."

"But—"

"Yes, but, Kühn attributes these two forms to two types of societies. One, he labels the 'parasitic society'; the other the 'symbiotic society.' The parasitic society is based on hunting, empire, and capitalism, while the symbiotic society is agriculturist, self-sufficient, and mutually beneficial."

Dorothy is about to ask a question, but Shale raises a halting hand. "It is my position that the sensory, naturalistic style represents the male principle, while the imaginative, symbiotic style is imbued with the female principle. In the SHE Cave, the Great Room, with its galleries, is the work of male artists, while the grottos are the work of female artists."

Shale lets her companions absorb these ideas while she fills a small, blackened pot with water from a canteen and sets it on a flat stone amidst the flames of the campfire.

"If this is so, what will we see in the grottos tomorrow?" Sheila is making it clear they will be kept out no longer.

"Nothing imitative on the walls. No representation of animals, nature, or humans. As for imaginative figures, those reside within you, in your mind's eye. There are some abstract forms, their meaning unknown, although I invite you to speculate now that I have documented them. Entering the grottos means leaving preconceptions behind. Your mind must be completely open and receptive."

Shale rises and takes a small tin box from one of the many pockets in her field jacket. From the tin, black tea is mixed with hot water in the pot. "Help yourself. Unfortunately, it is just good old Chinese tea, nothing transcendental, you know, for the sake of preparation." She gives them a wry smile.

They all stop, tin cups in hand and stare at Shale.

"There is a touch of the trance about the grottos. Small caves have a way of altering sensory perception."

Quiet descends, they sip their tea and listen to the night-hunting birds. Shale is still amazed by the lack of animal activity here. Certainly, there is the scurry of tiny creatures, but unlike the mountains of her childhood, there is no wolf song or bear snorts. The descendants of the cave bears have not put in an appearance. She has seen ibex and the retreating black-tipped tail of a lynx, but nothing larger.

"Well, Dr. Castro, what did you actually see?" Dorothy has yet to be mollified.

"As it happens, Miss Livesay, not much. Three white columns, floor to ceiling, bearing charcoal triangles suggesting eyes and noses— stalagmite statues."

"Geometric shapes. Is this common?" Dorothy's question is aimed at Shale.

"It is—right through to the Neolithic."

"And where are we?" Sheila asks. "New Stone Age, Old Stone Age, something in between?"

"My estimation—Upper Paleolithic. Late Stone Age roughly speaking from forty thousand to ten thousand years ago."

"No, that's inconceivable. I can't imagine that much time." Pat looks startled. "And the paintings—how can they exist after all that time? No, there must be some other explanation."

"Well, the caves are a very stable, protective environment, especially if they have been sealed by rock fall that has also diverted flowing water from the site. The entrance, as we know it, may have been closed for a long time."

"I thought Stonehenge was the oldest—"

"Neolithic, Pat. Young in my world." Shale looks passed Pat

to where Dorothy and Sheila are lifting the stew pot off the fire.

Alexandre douses what's left of the campfire with tea from the pot. Shale collects the tin cups and they all walk back toward the mine.

Once their camp utensils are stowed in the miners' cupboard, they drift toward the mineshaft opening and bed. Shale holds Alexandre back on the pretense that she would like him to look at the miners' tools, still piled at the back of the cupboard. Can he tell her the vintage of the tools? She explains that she is trying to reconcile the period of the mine site with the date of the letter she found in the Smithsonian. Are these the original tools of the 1880 mining operation, or has there been later work on this mine site?

Once the others have lost interest in her question, the women move off quickly to their bedrolls.

Shale is left alone with Alexandre to raise the real issue. "Dr. Castro, I have real concerns about the health of my friends, especially young Pat. These women need proper food and rest. And you and I know, your brother will not provide this when we return to the Palacio."

"What would you have me do?"

"Speak to him, at least."

"Do you believe that my entreaties will move El Comandante?"

His tone of voice is all she needs. "No. We need a carrot for the ass."

Alexandre chuckles. "The welfare of your friends is of no concern to my brother. You are the prize. The Smithsonian needs to put money on the table with a promise of more. Convince your Dr. Abbot that you are close to completion, that we will return only once more to the caves."

Shale cannot see his face in the dark, but he seems very sure of himself. "You have a plan?"

"When we hike down the mountain to meet the truck, we will not be going back to the Palacio."

"What of the guards?"

"They will obey me. They have no reason not to. We are going to drive to our family hacienda to be fed properly and recover."

"Thank you."

"From the hacienda, without the presence of the spying priest, we will call Dr. Abbot and convince him to send a BIS to the Bank of England."

"England?"

"My brother may see himself as a big fish in a small pond. He may be hedging his bets and ingratiating himself with the Fascists, but when it comes to money, well, let's just say he's of an international mind. He's had bank accounts in Switzerland and England for a very long time."

♋♋♋

Silently, they follow Shale down the left passage to what she refers to in her notes as the "Death Grotto." They are allowed into the entrance, no farther. Wide-eyed they look around.

"Oh, is this all there is?" Pat sounds profoundly disappointed.

"Pat, you first." Shale takes her by the hand and leads her to a depression in the clay of the cave floor. "Sit in the oracle's hole."

"The what?"

"Humour me—just my name for this concavity in the floor. It's about the width across of the female pelvis. You see it, don't you?"

"Yes."

"Now sit and face the wall closest to you."

"Okay, but there are no pictures just patches of colour."

"Remember what I said? The pictures are in your mind. The wall and its pigment stains are your canvas. Be still and focus." The others stand, barely breathing, at the cave opening.

"Oh, oh my, it's—"

"Don't tell us. We'll compare visions later."

With the exception of Shale, they all take a turn in the oracle hole. Then Shale asks them to examine the walls more closely.

"What are we looking for, Dr. Clifden?"

"Just take note."

They move silently around the small space peering at the floor, walls, ceiling.

"I'll pass my notebook around with the request that you write a short paragraph describing your observations."

"There are marks on the ceiling. Red lines, circles, other doodles—" Pat points here and there.

"Signs?" Sheila is staring at what she thinks is a row of spirals, zigzags, half-circles, dots and multiple lines.

"And what are these—these slots in the wall?" Dorothy slides her fingers into a thin vertical opening in the least concave of the walls.

Shale reaches into her knapsack and retrieves a wooden box with a faded label announcing Stag Horn Cigars, the beautiful image of a red deer echoing the wall paintings in one of the galleries.

From the box she removes a large linen handkerchief. Unfolding it carefully, she reveals what appears to be white tablets marked with hieroglyphics. "These are female skull bones, parietal bones to be precise, with charcoal impregnated engravings. The signs you are observing on the ceiling are engraved on these bones. The slits Dorothy pointed out in the wall held these bones for tens of thousands of years."

"A kind of mail slot." Pat looks from one to the other of the small band of explorers assembled inside a mountain. Delighted with her depiction, she sticks her hand into a nearby slot. For a moment her hand seems stuck there, then she aligns her fingers to release the rock's hold on her.

"Surely, this is fakery. Bones in slots? Next thing you're going to tell us is that these signs are written language." Dorothy looks askance at the walls.

"That's exactly what I'm saying. These signs and others have been found at Paleolithic sites throughout Europe."

"Given that they are a common occurrence—" Alexandre speaks for the first time since they entered the Death Grotto. He has been intent on studying the women's reactions to this small painted cave. "—why is the discovery of this room so important to you?"

Shale examines Alexandre as she tries to decide how much to reveal. "I discovered the SHE Cave and the grottos in May of 1934. During that field trip, I photographed the grottos thoroughly and removed the engraved bones. I photographed the Great Room and galleries, as well I dug a small initial pit in the Great Room floor and collected bone fragments and teeth. Similarly, I excavated the floors in these two passage grottos. I took this data back to the Smithsonian for examination and in-depth documentation."

"If that's the case, why did you return?" Alexandre suspects that there had to be a compelling reason for Dr. Clifden to return in the face of civil war.

"My samples convinced me and Dr. Abbot that I had found the beginning of written language. This is more than signs, more than code. Here, the arrangement of these ancient symbols follows prescribed patterns in the way words create sentences. It was imperative I find and document all the patterns, essentially the syntax."

"But now?" he asks.

"This is a monumental discovery. These women were creating human writing. If what they have left us were to be damaged or destroyed—the loss. It would mean a significant void in the search for what we human beings have become." Shale gathers up the engraved skull bones from the hands of her friends, reminding herself that time is short. "No other living being has the ability to represent an idea with an abstract sign."

"You are dedicated to a fault, Dr. Clifden."

"By October 1934 the political storm was on the horizon. The first clap of thunder was the miners' revolution in Asturias. Then the right-wing military uprising against the Republican government, and rebellion after rebellion as the Nationalists marched north. Dr. Abbot and I decided I should move fast and get in and out ahead of the Nationalists." The lantern has started to sputter. Shale looks around the Death Grotto at the women, her new friends, envisioning them on the rough Atlantic waves, vomiting over the side of the fishing boat as they made their way to Spain with her.

"Am I to understand that you were smuggled into Spain?" Alexandre is on a fishing trip of his own.

"Of course, not. We are papered and here legally." Shale wonders at his question.

"How old is the writing?" Pat asks. "As old as the paintings in the Great Room and galleries?"

"Yes. I authenticated the animal paintings, the handprints, and signs on my first field trip. As I said before, these caves date to the Upper Paleolithic."

"How did you authenticate the caves?" This is from Sheila.

"Come along and I'll show you." They follow Shale to the cavern. "Here, this giant deer."

"I thought that was a camel." Pat points at the hump.

"The hump is the giveaway. Recognizable animals during this period were larger than they are today. The Megaceros's or giant deer's neck ended in a hump of muscle between the shoulder blades. Most likely a result of larger, heavier antlers." Shale moves closer to the wall. "The artistic technique is typical of this period—a line drawing in black, either charcoal or manganese dioxide, in profile—the legs undefined and minimal shading overall."

Shale reaches into a deep pocket in her jacket. She hands Pat a magnifying glass. "If you look closely at the painted lines, you'll see infinitesimal spaces where the paint and rock have eroded. Even in the shaded areas on the neck and hump where the paint is heavier."

"Yes, that would suggest time has passed, but not how much time, surely." Dorothy takes the magnifying glass from Pat.

"The fossil record reveals that megafauna, the giant animals, including the cave bears, died out at the end of the Upper Paleolithic, the close of the Ice Age. Geology tells us that this occurred about twelve thousand years ago."

"That means all the bones scattered around are . . . incredible." Pat's eyes dart to the corners of the cavern.

"Along with erosion, the overlay of concretions and calcite also indicates age."

"What are these overlays? Can you show us?" Sheila looks around.

Shale turns toward a magnificent rendering of a bison bull. "See this reddish stain that has flowed down the wall and across the bull's flank, that is calcite. But, perhaps the most telling, the best timepieces are the stalactites and stalagmites. Look up at the stalactites—the ones hanging from the cave bears painted on the ceiling. Those huge pendants have been created by mineralized water, drop by drop. And the stalagmites—" Shale walks under the cave bear ceiling and stands between two pillars rising from the floor. They are desert brown and have the majesty of ancient Egyptian columns. "The stalagmites grow upward from drops of water hitting the floor. You can well imagine the thousands upon thousands of years it takes. Experiments indicate that they grow less than ten centimetres every thousand years."

"What of the grottos, Dr. Clifden?" Alexandre accepts the magnifying glass from Sheila.

"The grottos exhibit stalagmites such as those guarding the Death Grotto. More importantly the signs on the walls and the bones have been engraved before pigment was added. Again, if you magnify the engraved lines you will see what millennia have done in the form of micro-crystallizations. A newly etched line will be clean and clear. Not so prehistoric engravings. The lines are filling in, even as we speak. Time does not compromise."

Magnifying glass in hand, Alexandre moves from wall to wall. "These paintings and engravings seem fresh. Cleaner than many of the ancestral portraits that stare down from the walls of Casa de Castro."

"There is no proof these caves were inhabited. I have found no middens." Shale sees the look on Pat's face. "No refuse piles, no garbage holes."

"Which means?" Alexandre looks at Shale through the magnifying glass.

"No smoke from cooking and heating fires. No moisture from damp clothing, damp bodies, breath. The only significant damage to the walls is from cave bear claws."

"What of the other grotto?" Dorothy has not forgotten.

"We'll go there now." Theirs is the right state of mind for her experiment, Shale thinks.

As they reach the end of the passage, it becomes apparent that the entrance to this grotto is hidden by a bank of stalactites: ceiling to floor pipes reminiscent of an organ, except here the edges of the pipes are chipped.

Passing this stately array, Shale leads her party into a cave slightly larger than the Death Grotto.

"Oh my, have we entered a brothel?" Pat covers up a giggle with a well-placed hand.

"The red room," Sheila says.

"The Birth Grotto," Shale enlightens them.

"Yes, red ochre over black walls . . . I suppose the walls echo birth," Dorothy adds.

Alexandre turns to Shale. "Why do you call it the Birth Grotto?"

"Signs and bones" is her answer.

"Yes, I see the signs." Sheila points to rows of what look like incomplete triangles, point down and open, rendered in black.

"I excavated the floor on my previous trip. I found the remains of stillborn children."

"Remains?"

"Small skeletons, the bones not fully formed."

"A triangle for each empty womb, do you think?" Dorothy looks devastated.

"We can only surmise." Shale does not want them to linger with death. "Buried with the bones were pipes."

"Pipes?" Confusion replaces anguish.

"Yes, the musical kind, like flutes. Made from wing bones of such birds as vultures, geese, golden eagles. Bone bird flutes like this one." Shale slips a clean white tube from her pocket. Both ends are open, and there are three equally spaced holes running the length of its six inches.

"Is this from here?" Alexandre seems skeptical.

"No. This is a replica made from the wing bone of a domestic goose." Shale raises it to her lips, then appears to change her mind. Lowering the bird-bone flute, she points to depressions in the cave floor. "Please turn to the walls, find a set of indentations in the floor, place a foot in each hollow, and then squat."

After much scuffling, Shale retreats to the grotto opening. She places her lips on an open end of the bird-bone flute and blows while vibrating her lips. The sound, a primeval scream, becomes many screams echoing off the walls, wrapping them in pain. The red ochre rock vibrates before their eyes. Then suddenly, the screams are replaced by chimes—the ringing around them dispelling the red mist. Almost as one they turn to the entrance, Shale has gone, yet the chimes ring on.

They find her striking the stalactite pipes with a stick. The sound in the passage is less intense than the grotto, more harmonious.

"What just happened?" Sheila asks.

"You tell me?" Shale turns to them, expectant.

"I need to sit down." Pat slips to the floor.

"You traumatized us," Dorothy accuses.

"There is trauma, yes. But is that all?" Shale looks from one to the other, then strikes a single note on the pipes. A bell-like sound releases them.

"An opening . . . I saw light," Pat says.

Sheila lowers herself to the floor beside Pat and puts her arm around the younger woman's shoulder. "I wanted to run away," Sheila says.

"Yes, me as well." Dorothy sits on Pat's other side.

"What of your light, Pat?" Shale is pleased they want to talk about the experience.

"The wall opened up and there was a ball of warm, dense light."

"Did anyone else experience light?"

"I did." A surprising admission from Alexandre, who is traditionally the observer. "Sparks of light as if a flint had been struck to create fire."

Shale is pleasantly surprised that Dr. Castro would contribute. It speaks to the power of sound on the human psyche.

"What does it all mean?" Dorothy is studying the stalactite pipes from where she sits.

"Given the presence of flutes, the purposeful markings, and wear on the stalactites, and most importantly your experiences, I believe this grotto was a place of trance."

"To what end?" Alexandre asks.

"Communion, mitigating loss—any and all of the human emotions. This is not a reasoned approach to life and death."

"What are the markings on the pipes?" Dorothy gets up to have a better look.

"They seem to correspond to where sections of stone have been removed along the edges." Shale points out. "These adjustments appear to change the tone when the stalactite is struck near the symbol."

"You mean pieces of the edge were deliberately broken off?"

"Yes, the black lines and red dots are as purposeful as the precisely removed chips."

"This all seems rather fanciful." Alexandre is ambivalent and somewhat embarrassed by his participation in the Birth Grotto experiment.

Shale hands Alexandre the stick. "Here, strike the pipes first near the red dots and then the black lines. You don't have to believe me, believe your own ears."

The pipes sound frighteningly beautiful, confirming Shale's observation.

"Time to go. Gather up all your things from the Great Room. We leave tomorrow."

"Really? Down the mountain?" Pat seems disappointed.

"Yes, the truck will meet us," Shale discloses.

The women groan. While they are on the mountain, they feel free and safe.

"We will go to my family's hacienda where you can rest and eat wholesome food." Alexandre hopes they will recover quickly and become strong.

"A horse ranch?" Sheila asks.

"Yes. Horses are bred and the land is farmed. So, you see, you will eat well."

"Can we ride?" Sheila's spirits seem raised by the prospect.

"Why, yes, that can be arranged. You all know how to ride, I believe?"

Shale wonders at this question. It seems overly casual.

"I don't, not really," Dorothy says. "We had a pony for a time when I was a small child."

"I'll teach you," Pat offers, excitement building. "Sheila and I can teach you. You'll love it."

☙☙☙

The last of the food is eaten, making their burden lighter for the trek down the mountain tomorrow. The campfire provides comfort. The nights seem to be getting colder.

They settle in with their tin mugs of tea. Sheila and Pat are discussing how the grottos were painted, attempting to figure out what tools the women would have used. Finally, Pat asks Shale to enlighten them.

"Recall the texture of the grottos' walls. It is the result of pads made from moss or bison hair. Interestingly, on close examination, it appears the Birth Grotto was painted with bison pads only, while the Death Grotto was daubed using moss and lichen pads."

"How can you be sure?" Dorothy asks.

"There is bison hair and particles of moss and lichen trapped in the paint."

"However they managed it," Sheila adds, "it's very effective."

"With that thought in mind, I would be pleased if you would share your visions with me—what you saw when you sat in the oracle hole and stared at the wall." Shale quietly slips a notebook and pencil from her jacket pocket.

"Oh, well, let me see." Sheila raises her eyes to the clear night sky.

Over the next hour, as each took a turn, Shale recorded primarily animal images, no skulls, no bones, and only the occasional human face or figure, these primarily from Alexandre.

"And what of the Birth Grotto?" Shale finally asks.

She is assailed with auditory images from the sound of a flock of frightened birds to the snarls of back-alley tomcats to wailing women at an Irish wake. Again, Alexandre surprises her when he recounts the bawling of ambulance sirens and the screams of terrified children. It reminds her that she has yet to ask him how he had managed to make it out of Madrid. When she contemplates his escape, she imagines a well-planned, well-executed exit. She studies him across the campfire, and decides he is a man who is never without a plan.

Closing her notebook, she rises, gathers up each mug, and thanks each owner for believing in her quest and being here in the mountains with her.

ᏇᏇᏇ

Their makeshift tunnel bunkhouse is unusually quiet tonight. The women can't help but feel they are returning again to the unknown. If they spoke to it, they all would agree that it is time to leave Spain. Time, yes—the wherewithal unknown.

Shale understands her friends' reluctance to leave the mountain. Even the profound darkness of the mine tunnel is reassuring. She is still amazed by these women: their willingness to follow her into danger, their ability to work hard without complaint, their camaraderie. And yet, they are very different people. Certainly, all solidly middle-class Canadians, but with very different roots: journalism, medicine, and the military. The common denominator is an independent spirit. And Pat . . . so young and still ready to take on the world. Sheila has tasted the freedom of the frontier, while Dorothy has already seen enough injustice to make her a fighter, a radical. As for Spain . . . Shale's mind trips over this phrase. Rescue . . . what does it look like, whose face is it wearing? Dr. Abbot, the Smithsonian, the American government . . . they are a world away. No, it is up to her. Can she trust The Brother? What of his plan to have the Smithsonian ransom them? Seemingly his motive is to save his grandfather's collection, but she suspects he might also be planning to save himself, to somehow outrun Franco and the Fascists. Perhaps he also has bank accounts abroad . . . Switzerland, France, England, all possibilities. The Collection . . . the grandfather's collection is the bargaining chip. And with that thought holding back a flood of fear, she falls asleep.

4

HORSE TRADING

Ponferrada, Castilla y León, Gijón, Asturias

4

HORSE TRADING

Their excitement is contagious. Even the seasoned ranch hands are grinning as the women hang over the rail fence, whistling and calling to the horses in the paddock. Alexandre is encouraged: these Canadians are resilient. A bath, a farm meal, a night in a feather bed, and they are winning the hearts of his farm families by happily doing chores.

He motions to Shale and then turns to the herb garden at the back of the stone house. She follows without alerting the others.

"Do you need more time to complete your fieldwork, Dr. Clifden?"

"As always, I would like more time, but my documentation is sound." Shale waits on him to show his hand.

"We will call Dr. Abbot, secure a BIS transfer of payment for the Castro Collection and immediately leave for the Palacio, where you can select the pieces for the Smithsonian and I can arrange for packing."

"And what of El Comandante?"

"He will know of our call before we arrive. The walls have ears here, as well."

"Will he object?" Not even the redolent smell of thyme and basil can distract her from scrutinizing him.

"Oh, he will bluster until I tell him that the money will be deposited in his Bank of England account once the Castro Collection arrives in England."

"What does Dr. Abbot's deposit with the Bank for International

Settlements buy us?"

Alexandre looks around as if searching for shade and directs her to a bench in an open space at the end of the garden.

Once seated and convinced they are not being overheard, he says, "Time."

"To do what?" Shale wants the whole story.

"To make another trip to the cave."

"That would be wonderful, but not necessary." She wonders at his motives.

"Oh, it's necessary to keep you out of Octavio's clutches until the boat arrives in England, a Smithsonian representative takes possession of the Castro Collection, and the Bank for International Settlements transfers the payment to Octavio's account."

Shale looks him in the eye. "That's all well and good, but it does not mean El Comandante will release us. In fact, quite the opposite— he will have the Smithsonian's money and us."

"That is why we will escape."

"Escape! How?" Shale has managed to keep her voice a whisper.

"Let me just say, I have a plan. It is best you know nothing of it until we are back on the mountain."

Shale has been watching him closely. Now she holds his gaze long enough to search for signs of a lie. Then she realizes, he had said "we." "You are leaving, as well?"

"Yes, without me, you won't get very far."

"Is that the only reason?"

"No. My country is tearing itself apart and there is nothing I can do about it here. There are organizations outside of Spain who want what I want."

"And that is?"

"Peace and democracy."

They sit quietly taking in the beauty of the countryside overlaid with laughter coming from the paddock.

Eventually, Alexandre says, "By the way, make sure that you and the others keep your papers on your person and well hidden at all times. Even when you sleep—especially when you sleep."

"Papers?"

'I assume all of you took your identity papers and passports from your hiding places in the cave and have them with you."

"Is that all?"

"Whatever you do, don't tell your friends what I told you. All they need to know is we are going back up the mountain once they are rested and you have spent a few days at the Palacio cataloguing the Castro Collection."

"Well, from the sounds of it, my friends will be well entertained here. It seems they've taken to ranch life." Shale's tone alerts Alexandre that she is looking for reassurance.

"They will be safe and well cared for. I grew up with these people. While Octavio has always played 'jefe' here, the hacienda has been my true home." Alexandre rises. "We should go to the house and make our call to Dr. Abbot. I think our timing is right. Then we leave for the Palacio.

෬෬෬

Alexandre parks the truck and escorts Shale to the library. He searches out a leather-bound notebook that contains his grandfather's inventory and notes on his collection. He gives it to Shale with a second notebook, unused and ready for her to document her choices on behalf of the Smithsonian.

He leaves her to her task while he searches for Octavio, not before glancing up at a decorative wooden panel above the bookshelves. There are no pin pricks of light leaking from a slit in the panel's centre— the priest is not at his spy hole, for the moment.

Alexandre marches down the hall, knocks once, and throws open the door to Octavio's office. César gives two sharp warning barks, then leaps at Alexandre. Paws planted firmly on the man's chest, César gives Alexandre a wet slap across the mouth with a friendly tongue.

"Good thing he likes you, Xandre, although I don't know why."

"It's because I smell of horses."

"So I hear."

"What else have you heard?"

"Stop with the games." Ocho snaps his fingers. César immediately abandons Xandre to take his place beside his master's desk.

"The Smithsonian has agreed to buy selected items from grandfather's collection." Xandre pats César as he passes to the window where he sits on the stone sill.

"Buy, indeed." Ocho must turn in his chair to regard his brother.

"Yes, the BIS will transfer payment to your account when the Collection arrives in England. I need your Bank of England account number to make the arrangements."

"Bank of England," Ocho says quizzically.

"Wipe that supercilious look off your face. Do you really think I don't know about your bank accounts?"

"And what of the Smithsonian's spy?"

Xandre laughs so hard the mastiff abandons his post to sniff Xandre's feet.

"An American scientific institution is spying in Galicia. Good God, rational thinking has departed."

Ocho is unfazed. "An American—the United States has spies everywhere. But, of course, you know nothing of politics, you in your ivory tower."

"I know what anarchy is. I know we must protect what our ancestors have given us."

Ocho gives Xandre a long look. "The question remains—what of these women?"

"Dr. Clifden requires one more week to finish her work. She must then report back to Dr. Abbot. He will not release the money to your account until he hears from Dr. Clifden that they have left Spain."

"I knew there was more to it."

"Be that as it may, the Smithsonian's and Dr. Abbot's first priority is the women. He made that crystal clear."

"And how much money are they worth?"

"More than a nod from the Fascists." The stony look in his brother's eyes is not lost on Xandre, "Fifty-thousand U.S. dollars." The blood drains from Ocho's face as Xandre thought it would.

"No woman is worth that." Ocho starts to pace the room, the mastiff at his heels.

"These people have principles."

"And deep pockets." Ocho stops at the office door. "Let's eat."

"I'll collect Dr. Clifden." Xandre rises.

"No, leave her to her chore. I'll have the cook send a tray to the library."

No doubt César will be better fed than Shale, Xandre thinks as they walk down the hall to the dining room, the dog between them. Without missing a step, he realizes he has thought of Dr. Clifden as Shale.

ᖖᖖᖖ

The next morning Alexandre knocks on the bedroom door before unlocking it. A carving knife dangles from the door handle, left there by Octavio when he locked the door. Alexandre wraps the knife in his handkerchief and slips it into his jacket pocket. Released, Shale joins him in the hall.

As they walk to the library Alexandre asks, "Did you make much progress yesterday?" He does not want them to linger at the Palacio.

"Yes, your grandfather kept superb notes, even his handwriting is legible. I chose from his inventory and have gathered up at least half of the suitable artifacts. I've arranged them on and around the desk."

"Bravo. I will send the housemaids to dust and wrap your selections in newspaper. As we speak, the caretakers and gardeners are building wooden crates for me."

"How long will it take before we can pack?" Shale asks.

"The crates will be ready by tomorrow. Will you be?"

Shale has registered his sense of urgency. "Yes, even if I have to burn the midnight oil. I'm sure I'll have company. I heard snoring from behind the bookshelves around about siesta time yesterday."

Alexandre gives her a knowing smile. "Just so you know, I'm throwing in the cave bear skeleton from the attic. While you're working here today, I'll dismantle the skeleton and pack the bones."

They arrive at the library door. Alexandre grasps the handle, but does not open the door immediately. "As soon as the Collection is packed up, we'll load the truck and drive to Vigo. I'm sure you're familiar with the Port of Vigo."

Shale looks at the unopened door and nods.

ॐॐॐ

As they drive west, the closer they get to the Atlantic and the Porto de Vigo, the more traffic they encounter."

"Where are they all going?" Shale is astounded by the multitude of vehicles crammed with people, animals and possessions.

"Portugal. It means Franco is closer than I thought."

As they enter Vigo, it is clear that many of the travellers are headed for the Port.

Alexandre drives down Rua Real to the wharf, passing the Church of Santa Maria, and squeezing by cars and trucks parked in front of fishermen's houses. There is much haggling to be seen, and it has nothing to do with the price of fish.

They park and Alexandre leaves Shale in the truck as he enters the Port Authority Office to secure transport for the crated Castro Collection. When the forms have been completed and the paperwork handed over to Alexandre, the port officer will excuse himself to surreptitiously place a call to Octavio with the details. This is what Alexandre expects and desires. It reinforces his plan.

Outside, he stops at the top of the stairs to survey the wharf. The fishing fleet is in: the Vigo steamers, the first-ever small, steam-powered fishing boats, and most probably the type that brought Dr. Clifden and her friends to his shore.

Once the crates are loaded onto a freighter bound for Southampton, Alexandre suggests they have a meal before driving on to the hacienda. He is hoping his favourite café in the Plaza de Pedra is open.

They take one of the tables arranged under a stone archway that looks out on the square. The honey-coloured stone buildings surrounding the plaza are all of a type: three to five storeys high, with arched walkways at ground level and wrought iron balconies above. Compared to Rua Real, the Pedra is sedate, occupied by oyster sellers and housewives with shopping baskets.

With a splash of sun on her face, Shale seems relaxed to

Alexandre. There it is again: the familiarity that comes with a first name. "Shall I order the oysters? They're local, fresh and fabulous." He laughs at his choice of words and so does she.

"Do you think we can do away with formality?" he asks. May I call you by your given name and you mine?"

"Considering that we are planning to become outlaws, I think it is only fitting. Please call me, Grace."

Alexandre turns from his contemplation of the menu board. "Not Shale?"

"Certainly, if that's what you prefer."

"But, I thought—"

"Oh, I see. Grace is my first name, while Shale was given to me as a nickname, a childhood moniker the Walcott family had great affection for, so it stuck."

"Charles Doolittle Walcott of the Smithsonian?"

"Yes, he did fieldwork in the Canadian Rocky Mountains near the railroad town I lived in. My father helped with collecting and I helped clean the specimens."

"Is this how you became The Smithsonian Child?"

"In a manner of speaking. My father and Dr. Walcott became friends, both widowers at the time, and when my father died in an accident, the Walcott family took me in."

"It would seem you lived up to your name."

"Grace or Shale?" There is a mischievous light in her eyes, which turns to shadow when the waiter appears.

"What do you care for?" Alexandre asks Shale.

"The catch of the day would be a God-given luxury."

He nods at her reminder that while in Spain, she has not eaten well, and he orders a banquet for them.

They sit silently sipping their wine, aware they don't know each other.

Shale breaks the impasse, "Did you have a practice in Madrid?"

"No, I was solely an academic doing research at the university." He looks away across the Pedra.

"Research?"

"Behaviour modification," is Alexandre's concise answer.

It is Shale's turn to look out over the plaza. Finally she says,

"It was imperative you leave Madrid." A flat statement full of implications.

"The Republican government fled and so did I. The University City campus was a battleground." Alexandre's reply is matter-of-fact. "We, my colleagues and I, burned our notes and research papers, drove during the night, hid during the day, and stole petrol along the way to Santander. We needed to get to the coast and find a boat crossing to France. Professor," Alexandre pauses, "Professor X sent his family to live in Bordeaux months ago."

"You chose to stay." Shale wonders what has kept him in Spain, when clearly he has resources and could have left from Santander.

"Both my colleague and good friend Dr. Z and I decided to come home. He has aged parents in León."

Shale is tempted to ask what Alexandre had to come home to? He is saved from explaining his choice by the arrival of the food. Instead, Shale changes the subject. "You burned your research. Am I to understand that what you know could be dangerous in the wrong hands?"

"Perhaps. Certainly damaging. It could be used to reinforce negative ideas and social behaviour." Alexandre is pleased to see that Shale is now distracted by the delicious meal she is devouring. He uses her obvious pleasure to steer the conversation away from his work by way of a discourse on traditional Galician cookery.

☙☙☙

Heavy traffic slows their drive to the hacienda. They are thankful for full bellies since they will miss supper by hours.

The next morning Alexandre enters the kitchen to an uproar of voices and laughter. The women are assailing Shale with horse stories, in particular Dorothy's first ride across the pasture on a runner, the horse deciding the rider was not in charge. Miraculously, Dorothy had kept her seat and her head, riding the runaway to a walk.

Alexandre has heard enough and decides it is time to tell them they are riding back up the mountain.

After breakfast, Alexandre leaves orders for provisions to be packed and tack prepared. He has a lengthy discussion with the ranch foreman as they choose horses and assign riders. He then takes the coterie out for a stately ride among the hills so he can assess their ability for himself.

⊙⊙⊙⊙

They arrive at the trailhead as the sun is rising, viewed through the dusty windshield of an ancient touring car.

Alexandre's ranch hands had ridden the horses into the mountains the day before. They would drive back to the hacienda in the touring car, a rare treat considering the old Duke and Duchess of Alba had frequently occupied the touring car's leather seats.

The horses are ready, the saddlebags in place. And to Alexandre's surprise his old friend the foreman has also provided a mule to carry extra food, wine and bedding. The foreman had mentioned in passing that he thought Alexandre and his women were living like vagabonds, which was unacceptable.

They are in high spirits. The forest, which had been silent on their last hike to the cave, rings with their elation. It is agreed that the landscape is profoundly different from their vantage point astride a horse. Alexandre points out that they are probably seeing it for the first time. On the other occasions their eyes would have been locked on the trail to assure their footing.

As they continue on horseback, it is unnecessary to spend the night in the shepherd's hut, although it is dusk and they are bone-weary when they gain the summit and their mineshaft home. They make a fire to ward off the night and make a meal of bread, cheese, and wine. A standing meal that has Pat suggesting the wine has them adopting the stance of the ubiquitous cocktail party. As she rubs her backside, Dorothy disagrees wholeheartedly.

Alexandre watches as their saddle sores give way to banter about horsemanship. Finally, he joins in, "It would seem that Canadians are born to the saddle."

"A generation or two ago, perhaps," Sheila qualifies

his observation.

"You did very well today, Dorothy." Alexandre tips more wine into his tin cup.

"This is the first time you've called me Dorothy. Why now?"

"Well, Shale and I have decided that our escape is worthy of first names."

"Our what?" they demand in chorus.

"Tomorrow, we follow the Rio Sil to freedom." Alexandre expects them to sling questions at him, but there is only silence.

Dorothy turns to Shale. "Can we trust The Brother?"

"Yes, he has much to lose, more than we do."

The questions come, not as arrows but penetrating nonetheless. Surprisingly, they want to know who, not how. Who is he? They will not commit to the escape plan until they believe they can trust him.

By the time they spread out bedrolls, which smell of horse sweat, the women have agreed to ride down the northeast flank of the mountain to the Rio Sil Valley and on to Ponferrada. Alexandre cautions them that they will be finding their way off Serra de San Mamede through wild country.

ᏉᏉᏉ

Having emerged from the forest, Alexandre leads them to a rocky outcrop. They dismount before venturing out onto the precipice. Alexandre wants nothing more to do with rockslides and tangled undergrowth. He is grateful their Galician mountain ponies are surefooted – stumbling when broken rock gives way, only to regain their balance quickly.

To recover from the nerve-wracking descent, he suggests they sit on the outcrop and have a meal, at least some wine. As a civilizing gesture, he takes one of the blankets his foreman packed in the mule's pannier and spreads it on the rocks.

Once they are settled happily with food and wine, Sheila wants more than to simply gaze at the Rio Sil and the Aquilianos Mountains on the the horizon. She breaks the silence. "Tell us about Ponferrada,".

"What to say?" Alexandre pauses. "This place has a long history."

"Yes," Shale takes advantage of his mouth being full of bread and cheese. "Of course, there is the Templar Castle. But long before the Templar knights were charged with protecting the pilgrims on their way to Santiago de Compostela, the Astures—the Celtic peoples— built hill forts overlooking the river. And before that, there were settlements as far back as the Lower Paleolithic."

"You can't ignore the Romans." Alexandre has found his voice. "Emperor Augustus and the Astur-Cantabrian Wars of 29 to 19 BC. This region became the largest mining area in the Roman Empire."

"Still is, to its detriment," Shale adds.

"Say what you will, modern Ponferrada will aid us on our pilgrimage," Alex counters.

"I take it your plan doesn't include the Way of St. James?" Dorothy wants the details. She still finds it hard to completely trust The Brother. He plays his cards too close to his chest for her liking.

"No salvation for us in Santiago. Deliverance is ours." Alexandre sports a wry grin when he looks up at them. "Sorry, that was rather biblical."

"And just how is that going to happen?" Dorothy demands.

"By getting some rest."

"What, here on the mountain?" Her tone makes it clear she knows he is dodging her question.

"No, not without shelter. There's a hostel on this side of the river, on the road into town." Alexandre packs up the mule and they mount slowly, already stiff from tense hours spent in the saddle.

♋♋♋♋

"No, I'll do this on my own. All together we attract too much attention." Alexandre is adamant and impatient to leave for Ponferrada.

"Whose attention?" Who's watching?" Sheila is the inquisitor.

"No one yet. I want us far away by the time they come looking for us."

"You mean your brother?"

"Yes, of course, he'll be expecting us at the hacienda in less than a week."

"Away, where?" Dorothy has had enough of being kept in the dark.

"Far away. That's all you need to know for now."

"How do we know you'll come back?" Dorothy is relentless.

Alexandre looks her in the eye. "You don't. But ask yourself, why would I bother to bring you here only to abandon you? I could easily have got on a boat out of Porto de Vigo destined for France, as you well know. Retraced your route to Spain, as it where."

"Why keep us in the dark?"

"It's safer for all of us. Octavio's reach is far and wide." Alexandre leaves them standing at the hostel gate, as he rides away with the lead line in hand and the string of horses behind.

With Alexandre gone to Ponferrada, as planned the women shoulder their rucksacks, giving the impress they are trail walkers and leave the crowded, fetid hostel.

They follow the banks of the Rio Sil toward the foothills, a silent band of amblers until Pat breaks the tension. "We're outlaws. We need an outlaw name."

The declaration stops them in their tracks, all eyes on her.

"Well, jeepers. We can come up with something better than what they called us at the hacienda."

"What do you mean?" Shale demands.

"Tell her, Dorothy. You understand Spanish."

Dorothy looks from Pat to Shale. "You weren't there; I mean, you didn't hear them talking among themselves, calling us—Dr. Castro's harem."

"Well, better than some of the names they could have used." Shale is not smiling.

"Such as *puta*," Dorothy offers.

"Women in this society are either saints or sinners." Shale, having worked on digs at ancient sites, is well aware of how independent women are viewed. "But we're neither. So, yes, let's define ourselves."

"Okay, but nothing girly." Sheila stands with her hands on her hips, her posture defiant.

"Do we look like girly types to you? I, for one, certainly don't smell girly." Dorothy raises her arms above her head in a poor imitation of a languid stretch.

"It seems only fitting that we have the word 'gang' in our name." Pat seems firm on this requirement.

Shale lets her friends propose various titles, pleasantly surprised at how seriously they take themselves.

They walk on. Their mission is to stay away from the hostel and prying eyes.

♋♋♋

By the time they have finished their amble, the friends have not made a decision on a gang name. They turn to Shale.

"Well, since you've already put a name to our purpose in Spain, shall we call ourselves the SHE Gang?"

They all start talking at once, but what emerges, at least to Shale's ears, is that her suggestion couldn't be more fitting. Each and every one of them is nothing if not 'She'.

Their confabulation in front of the hostel gate is shattered by a blast from a horn. They turn indignant faces to the sound.

Alexandre pulls up in a battered car, the likes of which they've never seen. "Load your rucksacks, while I collect the panniers," he orders.

"Where'd you get the jalopy?" Pat asks.

He waves her through the gate on his way to the hostel.

On the road out of Ponferrada, silence reigns. It dawns on them that they truly are on the run. In the backseat, they can barely see out the small windows. Shale is up front with Alexandre. The dilapidated sedan fits right in on the rough country road.

Pat can only abide so much silence. "Alexandre, what kind of car is this? And did you find good homes for the horses? And where are we going?"

He glances at her in the rear-view mirror and decides less is more. "Well, for the curious among us, the car you're riding in is an Elizalde Tipo 48. Obviously well used, it's sixteen years old. I found it under a tarpaulin in the stable where I took the horses.

I decided it was perfect for us when I discovered it not only has an 8,143 cc straight-eight engine and four-wheel brakes, but a built-in tire pump. A lucky find. The horses and mule are with an old horse trader I know. He's a good man."

Alexandre is distracted by a line of tucks up ahead, approaching in the oncoming lane. "There are shawls in the seat pockets. Cover your heads and turn away from the windows. Act as if you're talking to each other."

He keeps his voice level and his eyes on the road. Shale has already wrapped herself in a black scarf.

Alexandre breathes more freely when they pull alongside and he realizes the trucks are loaded with farm workers, animals, and produce destined for the weekly market. He assesses the backseat in the rear-view mirror. The women look like the abuelas of his childhood, grandmothers shrouded in fringed shawls, but a force to be reckoned with. "I'm expecting to make Villablino by nightfall. We're going to stick to open country west of the Rio Sil, in the foothills of the Sierra de Ancares."

"Yes, but where are we going? Our destination?" Dorothy asks.

Dorothy reminds him of his father's mother, his no-nonsense, very grand, grandmother. "The coast."

"We seem to be travelling north. The Bay of Biscay?" Sheila surmises.

"Yes, El Golfo de Vizcaya is north."

"France, then," Dorothy pronounces. "But how? It's not like we can catch a ferry."

"Let me worry about that." And Alexandre is worried. Not only must they take on the dangerous waters of the Cantabrian Sea, but the city of Oviedo is held by the Nationalists. He had heard that the Siege of Oviedo ended when Fascist forces arrived. The capital of Asturias had become a Nationalist stronghold. Oviedo lies directly in their path.

"Why don't you trust us?" Pat asks outright.

"It's not about trust. Escaping Octavio is one thing, but there are Nationalists everywhere, not just in Franco's army. Across this country people have taken sides. You are either for the Republican government, which makes you a Loyalist, a Red, or a Leftist. Or you are for the Nationalist rebels, which makes you an Insurgent, a Fascist, a Rightist. That said, there's no way of knowing. Ordinary people don't have badges, don't wear uniforms. Sitting in a café, a cantina, you have no idea who is listening." Alexandre decides not to mention Oviedo.

"I take it, we won't be sleeping in a featherbed tonight?" is Sheila's assessment of Alexandre's lesson in Spanish politics.

Shale observes Alexandre's knuckles turning white as he grips the steering wheel. "We have the luxury of a canvas tent. I noticed it in the trunk when we were loading. Am I right, Alexandre?"

"Yes, the tarpaulin. If it rains," is his reply. "Otherwise, the stars will do just fine."

"Ah, camping," Sheila says with feeling. "I would ride my horse, Fiddle, into hills not unlike these. And then throw myself down anywhere for the night."

"Weren't you afraid?" Pat asks.

"Nothing too much to be afraid of. Fiddle and my dog, Juno, would alert me to nearby animals, including snakes. And I always carried a rifle."

"I missed that about home," Shale offers, "once I moved to the United States. That kind of freedom."

"So, Canada was always home, despite growing up in Washington?" Alexandre seems to have relaxed.

"Yes, the wilderness never leaves you. It makes you impatient with cities."

"That explains the role of archaeology in your life." Sheila nods in recognition.

"I would admit to a certain aversion to modern cities, but then I was a solitary child. My adoptive brothers and sister were adults when I joined the Walcott family. They were making their way in the world. And, of course, Mr. Wally spent much of his time in the field while I haunted the basement of the Castle."

"You lived in a castle?" Pat is in awe.

Shale turns to the backseat. "An American version of a castle— the Smithsonian Institution Building. Faux Norman style, twelfth century Romanesque and Gothic, but red, deep desert red—built with Seneca red sandstone from Maryland. We had an apartment on the second floor."

"But you were living in a museum. That's astounding," Dorothy says.

"You lucky duck." Pat punches the back of Shale's seat.

"Oh, I've got that beat." Sheila sniffs dramatically. "I grew up in an ivy-covered tower at a hospital, a lunatic hospital."

"Well, the Castro palacio pales by comparison. It would seem that I'm keeping exotic company." Alexandre sounds so earnest, but when they all laugh at him, he joins in.

"What profoundly unCanadian childhoods," Dorothy decrees.

"Not so," Sheila parries. "I'll have you know the New Westminster Hospital for the Insane had the best dairy farm in North America, so said the *Farmer's Advocate*. My father believed in work as a curative, especially working the land and caring for animals."

Alexandre catches Sheila's eye in the rear-view mirror. "Dr. Doherty appears to have understood his patients."

"From one professional to another." She nods a thank-you to him in the mirror.

"Tell me, Shale, how does one grow up in a museum?" Pat is still envious.

"By avoiding the scary exhibits—for that matter, by avoiding all the exhibits. That's why the basement became my domain. I carried a dictionary and learned the scientific words by decoding the labels on the storage boxes. The lids stayed on the specimen boxes marked 'shrunken heads,' 'spiders,' and 'the unborn'—the stuff of nightmares."

"You didn't have to go to school?" Pat can hardly contain the green-eyed monster.

"I had official and unofficial tutors. Teachers with lesson books and then those Smithsonian professionals who tolerated my constant questioning." Shale seems fond of these memories.

Alexandre is mesmerized, until he notices a car preparing to overtake them. "Abuelas," he says loudly. "Grandmothers, be grandmothers."

They adjust their shawls and lean away from the windows.

As an Hispano-Suiza in good condition passes, Alexandre gives the driver a friendly nod in the manner of the countryside.

"Well, Dorothy, it comes down to you and me, the quintessential Canadians," Pat declares.

Dorothy cannot hide her surprise. "How so?"

"Winnipeg is biblical—flood, wind and pestilence. Only the chosen survive the Red and Assiniboine Rivers, the Arctic winds, and the blackflies."

"You lived in Winnipeg?"

"My father was transferred to Winnipeg as second-in-command of Lord Strathcona's Horse. We lived in the barracks at Fort Osborne." Pat is precise with the history. "So yeah, I lived in a Fort. It was a dump. Nothing like those piles of stone sitting on the tops of hills around here."

"I was born in a snowstorm, first blizzard of the year, October 12, no less." Dorothy has always thought of it as prescient.

Alexandre points out one such ruined hill fort as they speed north encountering few vehicles, as he had hoped when he chose the route.

⤚⤚⤚⤚

Cresting a hill, they can see reflected light in the night sky. Below is Villablino, bright as a beacon. Alexandre decides it is a Siren. It is not the sleepy town he had anticipated—too much light, too many opportunities to be seen.

They descend and keep driving into the night. If Sheila, who seems to have a built-in compass, were awake, she would register that they are now travelling east rather than north. Alexandre is circumventing Oviedo by way of Mieres. He will rest just before they make their run for the coast and Gijón. Rest and reconnaissance.

The Siege of Gijón had ended months ago in August when Republican miners charged the Nationalist garrison held by Colonel Antonio Pinilla. The only weapon the miners had was dynamite. The barracks burned to the ground. As far as Alexandre knows, Gijón is still in Republican hands.

Navigating the Cordillera Cantábrica at night proves to be more of a challenge than Alexandre had foreseen. The unrelenting climb and sharp switchbacks take their toll on him and the Tipo 48. Steam pours from under the hood as Alexandre pulls off the road beside the Church of Santa Cristina. All he can do is turn off the Tipo and rest his forehead on the steering wheel. Except for the sound of hissing, total silence envelops them. The unlit church made of native stone looms like a Cordillera cliff.

"Pre-Romanesque, by the look of it." Shale considers the church a better subject than the car.

Finally, he looks up drawn by the sound of rain on the roof. "Welcome to the Hotel Santa Cristina."

"Really? Won't it be locked?" Pat asks.

"No. Sanctuary for anyone who needs it in these mountains."

The women grab their rucksacks and make a dash for the church entrance while Alexandre examines the mesh grille where most of the letters spelling Elizalde are missing, but the **E** medallion is proudly present. The cold mist and rain have begun to cool the pinging metal, but he thinks better of trying to open the massive hood. Instead, he takes long strides to the back of the Tipo, unfastens the lid of the leather box strapped to the frame and retrieves the panniers. Time to eat.

Having passed through the vestibule, Alexandre is stopped in the central nave by the sight of the women standing in a chancel that is raised above floor level. Each one is framed by an arch—as if they are statues placed in niches. The church is immaculate. There is a vase of flowers gracing the heavy blocks of craved stone that form the altar.

"Will it do?" he asks.

"How old is it?" Pat responds, question for question.

"I believe it was completed in the ninth century."

"There seems to be some borrowing here," Shale says. "A single rather than a triple apse, stone lattice between the arches—"

"Borrowing is a polite word, more likely looted from a seventh century Visigoth church, at least the lattice."

"I, for one, think it has a good feel." Pat lays out her bedroll on the platform.

"Yes, not as chilly as I expected it to be. The stone seems to have held the heat of the day." Sheila prepares her bed under the central arch leading to the apse.

"Just as long as the roof keeps out the rain, I have no complaints." Dorothy is unpacking the food pannier and laying out the contents on the altar. In mid-task she stops, a loaf of bread in hand, and turns to Alexandre. "I don't mean to insult you. By using the altar as a table, am I—?"

"Being sacrilegious," Alexandre finishes her sentence. He nods to the repast. "You've provided bread and wine, after all." Then he grins. "Please continue."

Gathered around the altar, they are thankful for the chance to stand after long hours spent in the car.

"Dr. Clifden, your knowledge of the past seems to encompass more than prehistory," Alexandre addresses her across the crumb-laden altar.

"Well, when I was simply Grace or Shale, Mr. Walcott saw to it that I received an excellent education.

Alexandre nods his head to acknowledge the reminder about titles and first names. "Vassar College as I recall."

"Your memory serves you well. I went on to Radcliffe College at Harvard University and then the University of Pennsylvania. I would have to say, my real education began when I became a member of a joint excavation at Mount Carmel. Exploration of the Wadi el-Mughara Caves undertaken by the British School of Archaeology in Jerusalem and the American School of Prehistoric Research. The director was the phenomenal Dorothy Garrod."

"Veritas, be told. Well, isn't that a coincidence." Alexandre's ironic tone is not lost on the group. "It would seem we are alumni. But then, you knew that."

"What is he talking about, Shale?" Dorothy's increasing frustration with unknowns, with puzzles, is apparent.

"Dr. Castro also attended Harvard University, and that's the truth. We certainly weren't classmates."

"Oh, I see. Association by degrees—" Dorothy pours more wine, while they all try to assess the intent of her words. "Well, don't just stand there, laugh, chuckle, chortle, something."

"Oh, very clever, Miss Livesay —Dorothy." Alexandre raises his tin cup of wine to her.

"Cheers." She touches his cup and smiles.

They seem to be on a better footing, Alexandre thinks. "What has your education taught you, Dorothy?"

She studies him over the rim of her cup. "Justice is an illusion. There is only power."

They all turn to look at her.

"Are you a nihilist?" Alexandre is the first to speak.

"I'm a realist." Dorothy surveys the stone church. "And history will bear me out. If these stones could speak, they would as well."

"Considering we are fleeing a power struggle." Sheila pauses.

"We are witnesses." Shale places her cup on the altar.

"That's the job of the artist," Pat says.

The gang turns as one to her. Their eyes make her nervous. "Paint, words, music all testify. We will tell this story in poetry and pictures."

"Hear, hear," Shale salutes. They all raise their cups.

☙☙☙

Rucksacks are packed and the women are preparing to leave the chancel. Alexandre climbs the stairs from the nave to the platform and approaches the altar. He lifts the heavy metal urn laden with flowers and places it on the edge of the platform. The others look on, puzzlement obvious on their faces.

Alexandre jumps down from the platform, removes the flowers from the urn and turns to leave with the metal vessel in his arms.

"Stop thief," Sheila says.

"Only the water" is Alexandre's curt reply.

"There is a well behind the church," she reminds him.

"The water in this urn is the right temperature." He is walking away down the centre aisle.

"Oh, of course, the radiator."

"Speaking of the well, we should fill our goatskin bags." Dorothy, always the practical one.

Alexandre meets them at the well, refills the urn and disappears into the church through an arched annexe that forms the south arm of the church's Latin cross construction.

The automobile is packed and they're ready to leave Santa Cristina to her mountain solitude, when Alexandre notices a figure in the rear-view mirror.

"Abuelas, quickly," he says in an undertone as he pushes open the heavy door.

Moving toward the rear of the Tipo, he extends his hand to the squat man dressed in black. "Father, fine morning."

"Yes, the rain has settled the dust." Having shaken Alexandre's hand, the priest looks to the automobile. "You're on your way then. Is your journey long?"

"Not very. We're on our way to visit our grandmother in Mieres del Camino."

"Ah, well, I won't delay you. That's a grand old automobile. My uncle owned one. I don't remember it having an inside mirror."

A keen eye, this priest. Alexandre is on guard. "Yes, the Argus dash mirror is a useful addition."

"I imagine so. Safe journey. You know, of course, there is still unrest and some fighting around Oviedo and Gijón."

"Yes, as far as I know, the storm has not reached Mieres."

"God bless." The priest turns to the church.

᎒ᏻᏻᏻ

The closer they come to Mieres del Camino, the heavier the traffic. Alexandre is relieved to see that it is primarily farm vehicles, and goods trucks. He had hoped against hope that they would not encounter army vehicles, at least, not yet.

Mieres should be bustling, but the streets are strangely deserted. He wonders if there is some kind of ban or curfew. Alexandre decides to stay on El Camino and drive through the city as fast as possible.

On the outskirts of Mieres the road divides: one branch is the way to Oviedo; the other branch will take them to Gijón.

Everything is still, as if the land itself is holding its breath. This torpor is more frightening than the sight of military vehicles, or so they think. Alexandre decides it is rare good luck and pushes on as fast as the Tipo's radiator will allow.

They barely acknowledge towns such as Langreo and Siero; they hold only the harbour of Gijón in their mind's eye.

As they enter Gijón, war is apparent, heralded by trenches cut in the hills and the burned out remains of Simancas Barracks. Flapping in the sea breeze is the tricolour Republican flag with its lion and castle crest standing proud on red, yellow, and purple bands. Alexandre is relieved, able now to focus on finding them passage to France.

Their progress is slowed by market stalls and shoppers. Alexandre spots a space between two farm trucks, their boxes enclosed by the addition of high, wooden sides. He turns off the main street and parks the Tipo in this convenient refuge. The SHE Gang is quietly apprehensive.

"I'll take the panniers to the market and buy provisions. We have no way of knowing how long we will be here, and it's not safe to dine locally."

"Oh, brilliant idea," Sheila says.

"And your choice of parking spot is uncanny," Dorothy adds with admiration.

"Nevertheless, keep your shawls in place"— his parting admonishment.

The women start to giggle. "We look a fright," Pat intones. "Not even my grandmother would approve of our state of dress. Mind you, she's English to the core." Pat pushes the shawl fringe off her face.

"Mine as well, a grand English lady." Dorothy seems pleased to speak of her. "But I think she would approve of our ruse. She volunteered for the war effort on the home front, and spent a goodly portion of the last war overseeing convalescent homes for wounded soldiers and setting up canteens for the city folk sent into the country to work on farms."

Shale is listening, but she is also thinking ahead, assessing Dr. Castro's ability to negotiate. This is a working port: the ships and their captains are not in the business of transporting passengers. Although she is sure the women of the SHE Gang are not the only ones trying to leave Spain. There are ways and means when there is money to be had, which raises another concern: Just how will they pay for passage if they find it?

Her friends have climbed the branches of their respective family trees, generating much subdued amusement. It has not gone unnoticed that Shale has not contributed to the tale-telling. Their unspoken assumption is that her family tree is lost to her. They move the conversation on to speculating as to what Alexandre will buy.

Before long, he arrives back with the panniers. He drops them into the leather box strapped to the back of the Tipo, relief obvious on his face. Before he secures the box, he lifts a colourful woven bag from one of the panniers.

Alexandre takes the passenger's seat in the front of the car and hands the bag back to the women. "Picnic—something I've only ever done in America. Do Canadians have picnics?"

"Only in the summer," Sheila says.

"Yes, of course."

They are kept occupied with fresh bread, goat cheese, and empanadas—small pies stuffed with sardines. The car smells glorious. Their own restaurant on wheels.

"Oh, I just about forgot." Alexandre reaches into his jacket pocket. He hands them each a small rectangle of needlework. "These are bookmarks, I'm told. A young woman makes and sells them in the market. She looked so thin and haggard—I couldn't pass by."

"They're lovely. Very well done. My mother used to work in petit point, until her eyes could no longer deal with the tiny tent stitches." Sheila admires the artistically crafted flowers and birds painstakingly stitched on stiff canvas.

"I didn't think anyone did this kind of tapestry needlework anymore. And you said she was young?" Dorothy asks.

"I discovered that her husband is a miner. He's away. Joined the CNT militias. They're in the mountains, securing the passes."

"Who are they? This CNT?" Pat asks.

"Confederación Nacional del Trabajo. Workers, mostly miners in Asturias. Republicans. Part of the assault on the garrison here in Gijón."

For the moment, the picnic is a respite from the realities of their situation. Eventually, they are sated, and Shale recognizes an opening. "Alexandre, what do you expect to find at the docks?"

"Foreign ships." He looks beyond them out the back window, to see if they are being watched.

"Do they come here often, even now?" Dorothy follows his gaze.

"Yes, Gijón is an industrial port. Asturias exports coal and steel. Imports oil."

Alexandre brings his focus back to what he's come to learn recently is the SHE Gang—a ridiculous title, as far as he's concerned. "Let's go take a look. Maybe we'll get lucky."

Alexandre backs out of their hiding place and pulls onto Gran Vía. After a few wrong turns, he manages to navigate the densely packed commercial precinct bordering the Puerto. Again he finds an out-of-the-way place to park the all too conspicuous Tipo 48.

Crossing the railway tracks, they find a vantage point from which to view the harbour. More important than the ships themselves are the flags they fly. They're in luck: there is a tanker and a freighter flying British flags as well as two small cargo ships under French flags.

They sit on the seawall to discuss their options and to decide on a plan of action. Until now, they had not considered sailing to England. Bordeaux had seemed to be their obvious destination.

Leaving the seawall, their intention is to approach the English captains first. In this case, Alexandre has been relegated to the sidelines. Shale, in her capacity as Dr. Grace Clifden, leader of a Smithsonian Institute archaeological expedition, will be their representative.

To reach the British ships, they must start the climb to Monte de Santa Catalina on the headland. As they gain elevation, they are able to see the breakwater and the inner harbour. The gang is stopped in its tracks by an explosion of shouts and cheers. The breakwater is crowded with a raucous throng waving Republican flags. The focus of their celebration is a Spanish freighter flying a huge Republican flag from its mast.

With so many people in the area, the gang decides to make haste for the British freighter. Luckily, the stone stairs leading down to the docks are free of bystanders, and the group makes its way quickly to the docked ship and its gangplank. There is no one posted to stop them from climbing onto the ship.

Once they gain the deck, a sailor approaches the group. "Hoy, where do you think you're going?"

Dorothy, affecting an English accent, answers, "Good day, we would like to speak with your captain."

"Would you now? Case you hadn't noticed, this is no passenger liner."

"Yes, rightly so. The captain, please." There is steel in her voice.

He looks them over. "Who are you?"

Dorothy has noticed the captain standing in the doorway of the deckhouse above them. She turns to Shale. "This is Dr. Clifden of the Smithsonian Institute of America. We were carrying out historic research when we were kidnapped by a Fascist governor."

The captain crosses to the bulwark, in order to look down on them. "How did you escape?"

Shale raises her head. "This is Dr. Castro of the University of Madrid." She places her hand on Alexandre's arm. "He came to our aid. On horseback, no less."

"Well, that sounds like a story worth hearing." The captain orders the sailor to show them to his quarters.

The room is comfortable if not spacious, and remarkably devoid of personal trappings. This is not where the man lives; it's where the man abides.

Arriving, he introduces himself as Captain Bill Williamson. "It would appear you're on the run."

"Well, with the exception of Dr. Castro, we are attempting to get home," Shale explains.

"And home is where?" He seats himself at the head of his table.

"Canada—for the three of us, " Dorothy says.

"I see you've lost your English accent, Miss."

"Miss Livesay. And I come by my accent honestly: my father is from the Isle of Wight, where my people still reside."

"And you, Dr. Clifden, am I to assume you are American?"

"Yes, but Canadian by birth. Washington, DC is my home now. That said, England would be a welcome port in this storm."

"It would seem that is not true for some of your countrymen."

"How so, Captain Williamson?" Sheila makes her presence known.

"The first units of the International Brigades have arrived in Madrid," he announces. "Had you heard this news, Dr. Castro?"

Alexandre silently stares passed the captain. "No, I didn't know. We have been travelling from Galicia."

"By horseback, it would seem." Captain Bill's look is quizzical. This elicits a grin from Pat.

"Not entirely. We rode for some days through the mountains until we found a town where we could trade our horses for an old automobile."

"Mountains, indeed. And how do a couple of doctors find themselves in the high sierra?" Captain Bill has made a pensive steeple of his fingers.

"I work in the area of prehistoric archaeology. I made a unique discovery here, in a mountain cave, and came to Spain with my field crew to quickly document this find."

"And yourself?" Captain Bill points his steeple at Alexandre.

"My university colleagues and I left Madrid rather than be forced to devise tortuous methods of extracting information from prisoners of war. I am a doctor of psychology."

"And the horses. How did you come by those?"

"They were mine. From the family hacienda."

"You left your home. Had the war reached you?"

"Yes, it came with my brother. He's a Rightist and an admirer of General Franco. Whereas, I am not."

"Ah, civil war. The enemy within. When countrymen take up arms against each other, the wound will be too deep to heal."

The cabin falls silent.

Captain Bill gives his head a shake and returns to the problem at hand. "Freighters are not devised for women."

"That could be said of much of the world." These are the first words Pat has uttered.

Captain Bill gives her a look that is both amazed and fatherly. "You sound like my daughter, the bluestocking."

Pat returns his look. "I would like to meet her." Pat's meaning is not lost on Captain Bill and the others.

"Indeed. Did you hear the brouhaha in the harbour?"

They nod.

"A Spanish freighter transporting international volunteers to fight for the Republic. It set sail from England when we did."

"Remarkable. Finally, The Cause is being taken up. There was talk when I left Canada, but no action." Dorothy is moved.

"The Cause . . . is it? I'm a man of action. I'll do my bit. Welcome aboard." Captain Bill looks closely at his guests. "Do you have luggage?"

"In the automobile," Alexandre says. "My canvas bag and panniers with some good food and decent wine."

"In that case, Dr. Castro, I'll assign a deckhand to help you retrieve your things—swiftly—don't linger. We sail within the hour." Captain Bill pushes his considerable bulk away from the table. "As for you ladies, we may not be a twelve-passenger freighter like some, but you are in luck. I'm sailing without a first mate, so his cabin is available. It will be a tight squeeze, but there you are." He straightens and gives them a stern look. "I have one request of you: Please do not leave the bridge. You have to remember this is a working ship." He contemplates each one in turn. "Do we have an understanding?"

The gang nods solemnly.

"Very well. That's the last speech you'll get from me. I'm a man of few words."

Pat gives him another grin.

Captain Bill heads for the door. "This way to your quarters." Suddenly, he stops. "Oh, Dr. Castro, you'll bunk with me. And I'll have a deckhand meet you at the gangplank."

☙❧

The Tipo 48 is hidden so well, that Alexandre is unsure of its location. The streets with their warehouses all seem the same. He hopes he is not showing the anxiety he feels as he casts about looking for familiar landmarks. The deckhand is Spanish, and Alexandre reassures him with an "Está bien."

He asks his helper to wait while he climbs the outside stairs of a nearby warehouse. Wryly, he thinks of the vantage point as his crow's nest. He doesn't spot the Tipo48, but he does recognize a brick building he passed earlier in his search for a permanent home for the stately Elizalde.

Alexandre remembers the captain's admonishment and clambers down the stairs. The deckhand has to stretch his legs to keep up with his companion.

Coming around the corner of the brick building, Alexandre remembers. A few more turns and they are at the automobile. His wide-eyed companion accepts one of the two panniers from the leather box and with Alexandre's fond thump to the old Tipo's back window, they're off with as much speed as the full panniers and canvas bag will allow.

♋♋♋

After hugs all around, the SHE Gang settles into the small cabin. They are almost too excited to realize that the room is more a closet than a cabin.

Dorothy gets to work moving furniture to make floor space for their bedrolls.

Having no coins or straws, they resort to the childhood game of rock-paper-scissors to establish who gets the berth as her bed.

Shale wins, but stipulates that she will only sleep in the narrow bed for one night. Then the SHE Gang will play at being children again.

They see neither the captain nor Alexandre before the ship creaks and groans its way out of the harbour. Not wanting to be underfoot, they have not ventured out of the first mate's cabin, but they are concerned about Alexandre's whereabouts. Finally, Shale decides to, at least, knock on the door of the captain's quarters.

Alexandre opens the door. "There you are."

"We didn't know if you had made it back."

"And I didn't know where you were."

"I'll just go and reassure the others, and then I want to talk to you. I assume you're alone?"

"Yes, the captain is in the wheelhouse."

Minutes later, Shale lets herself into the captain's cabin. Alexandre is seated at the table with a glass of wine. He has poured one for her."

"Come, join me." He rises to pull a chair out for her.

Shale examines the wine in the sturdy tumbler. "With everything, I had forgotten you had shopped at the street market."

"I think the captain is glad I had." He gives her a sly smile. "Saúde!"

She comes back with, "Cheers!"

"Practising at being English, are you?"

"I always liked that English salutation; it's so positive. And speaking of England: have you made plans? Will you stay in London?"

"Yes, I'll meet with the agent overseeing the Castro Collection. You should be part of that meeting, as well. Representing the Smithsonian, of course. We can do an inventory together."

Shale nods. "I also wanted to discuss payment for our passage. Doing one's part for democracy is all well and fine, but we believe Captain Williamson should also be compensated. That said, even combined, our funds don't amount to much."

"I have money enough to pay for our passage, and I also plan to offer him the Tipo 48. I know there are citizens of Spain among his crew; they will know what to do with the automobile."

"Oh, that's a fine idea." She looks askance. "I mean about the Tipo. As for our passage, once in London, I will make arrangements with Dr. Abbot to reimburse you."

"You already have." A roguish look crosses his face.

"How so?" Shale recognizes that Alexandre has something up his sleeve.

"My English agent has seen to it that the Smithsonian's payment for the Castro Collection has been deposited into my London bank account."

Shale laughs and raises her tumbler of wine. "You sly dog."

"Cheers," he says.

5

SIGNS OF THE TIME

London, Paris

5

SIGNS OF THE TIME

Shale and Alexandre are satisfied that the Castro Collection is intact and ready to be shipped to the Smithsonian. The London agent presents Alexandre with the papers, shakes his hand, and reassures Dr. Castro that he is at his service, now and for the future.

"Time to meet the SHE Gang for lunch." Shale takes Alexandre's arm as they step onto the busy London street.

"The 'gang'! I despise that sobriquet. Ladies would be preferable."

"Not to the 'ladies.' There's not a parlour in this world that could contain these young women. Those days are over. After all this is the home of women's suffrage."

"I see, then why are you holding my arm?" Alexandre expects to see signs of embarrassment on Shale's visage.

"Oh, well, that's obvious. I'm steering you in the right direction."

When the shock leaves his face, Alexandre laughs an honest laugh. "And just where are you directing me?"

"A pub lunch down the street from Canada House."

"Your old stamping ground?"

"You say 'stamping,' I say 'stomping.' And, yes, a celebration of sorts."

"What are we celebrating?"

"Freedom."

"A sign of the times. Not long ago we took freedom for granted," Alexandre reflects.

"No longer, not with Fascism on the rise across Europe. I heard from our concierge, that not long before we arrived, there was a clash between police and protesters in London's East End."

"Protesters?"

"Yes, Anti-fascists who meant to keep the British Union of Fascists from marching through Stepney. The residents took to the streets and threw up barricades."

"Why did the police get involved?"

"Because the Home Secretary refused to ban the Fascists' march, despite a petition against it with over ten thousand signatures." Shale gives her head a sad shake.

"My, you learned a great deal from our hotel's gatekeeper. How did the two of you come to this topic of discussion?"

"Gatekeeper Henry Horowitz enquired as to whether you were from Spain."

"Indeed, why would my place of origin be of any interest to him?"

Shale gives Alexandre a frank look of bewilderment. "The world is watching Spain. We escaped more than a civil war."

Alexandre does not seem convinced, so Shale continues, "Henry informed me that the protest is now called, the Battle of Cable Street. And the slogan, which can still be seen painted on windows, doors, and pavements, is No Pasarán."

Alexandre stops in the street to stare at her. "The battle cry of the Republican forces—No Pasarán—They Shall Not Pass—here, in the streets of London?"

"There is a great deal of unrest here. Mr. Horowitz made that clear for our sakes and safety."

Crossing Trafalgar Square, Shale slows their pace in order to give Alexandre the benefit of her nocturnal inquiries. Feeling unsettled by the night noises of the city, she has been unable to sleep and has spent the last few nights in the hotel's lounge, reading back issues of *The Times* and *The Telegraph*.

Intent on describing the Hunger Marches in London and the Jarrow Crusade, Shale passes a Greek Revival building, home of the High Commission of Canada, without a second look.

Alexandre interrupts her recitation to ask, "Isn't that building Canada House?"

"Yes, formerly the Union Club and the Royal College of

Physicians. Now turned over to colonial independence, such as it is."

"What do you mean?"

"The British class system is insidious. It is not only here on home ground that workers march, rally, and demonstrate against being slave labour. It was one thing to be fodder on the battlefields and in the trenches of Europe. There, men where protecting their homelands. In so doing, they learned their lives are worth something. But they returned to widespread unemployment and the failure of the capitalist system. So, here in England, two hundred unemployed men marched 291 miles from the shipbuilding town of Jarrow to London to deliver a petition to the House of Commons."

"And hunger marches?" Alexandre is mesmerized, more by the passion of Shale's delivery than the story itself.

"The unemployed have been demonstrating since the early 1920s. Even now, there are rallies in Hyde Park that often turn violent. The post-war slump and then the world recession—these are desperate people, living on air and little else for the better part of two decades."

"How can the powers that be ignore this situation?"

"They're busy building barricades against Socialism and Communism. They're protecting their right to the lion's share."

"Ah, that's why there are so many statues of lions in London."

Shale stops dead, letting go of Alexandre's arm and stepping back. She looks him over as if he has just approached her on the street. "And many statues of horses. But let me tell you, this is not a hobbyhorse—this is an outrage." She walks on.

"Grace, I meant no offence."

She is distracted by his use of her name, but not for long. "The harbour at Gijón, the cheering Spanish people on the breakwater. Do you think there were lions among those men of the International Brigades? Those Canadians and Americans who have come to fight for Spanish democracy are victims of the class system—unemployed and hungry for a place at the table. Everyone is entitled to a fair share."

Shale stops in the street again. Alexandre takes a step back, steeling himself against another lecture. "This is it." She smiles at his confusion. "The Dray Horse Inn." She points to the sign hanging above their heads.

Alexandre holds the door open for her. They enter the public house and find most of the SHE Gang at a table set between the windows and the fireplace. "Hello ladies, you look most comfortable." Alexandre avoids looking at Shale.

"Comfortable! You look terrific," Shale says. "A successful assault on the shops this morning by all accounts." She realizes Sheila is missing.

The women turn to each other nodding their heads at the transformation the new clothes have made. Against their protests, Shale had paid them from her Smithsonian bank account for their work at the SHE Cave.

"Not bad yourselves," Pat remarks. "It seems you found some very classy clothes before the meeting with your agent."

Shale surveys the plethora of empty glasses on the table. "Did you succeed in sending cablegrams home to your families?"

"Did and done." Pat points to the empty space beside her on the window seat. "We saw you arrive and Sheila and Hazen have gone to the bar for more drinks."

Alexandre and Shale both turn to look at the bar

Dorothy doesn't wait for their question. " Hazen Sise, we met him at Canada House. He's on his way to Madrid."

Despite herself, Shale manages not to look pointedly at Alexandre. "To join the International Brigades?"

"Certainly a select brigade. Are you acquainted with Dr. Norman Bethune?"

Both Shale and Alexandre shake their heads.

Dorothy continues, "Dr. Bethune has formed a Canadian Medical Unit. Hazen is to be his ambulance driver in Spain, where Bethune will set up a mobile blood transfusion unit for wounded Republican soldiers."

"This Dr. Bethune, he's going to the battlefields?" Alexandre looks incredulous.

According to Hazen, he'll drive the ambulance and Dr. Bethune to wherever the wounded are including where they've fallen."

Alexandre goes to the bar to introduce himself and help with the drinks, while Shale slides in beside Pat.

"Your new friend is most intriguing," Shale says as she studies her friends. It is difficult to believe that mere months ago, they were strangers, sitting here laughing, drinking, getting to know each other.

"Intriguing, yes, and a dreamboat." Pat raises an eyebrow, newly plucked and shaped that morning.

"Besides being the man of Pat's dreams, Hazen is an architect who has just met his conscience in the form of Dr. Norman Bethune." Dorothy adds.

"Okay, you two give me the straight goods." Shale glances at the bar where Hazen and Alexandre are deep in conversation.

"Dr. Norman Bethune, Canadian physician, surgeon, member of the Communist Party, anti-fascist, and humanitarian. And, it would seem, someone who expects to change the world." Dorothy, as a member of the Canadian Young Communist League, knows more about Dr. Bethune than her straight goods suggest.

"And this paragon is here in London?" Shale asks.

"Yes. Dr. Bethune has loaded a Ford station wagon to bursting with medical supplies. With Hazen behind the wheel, they're heading for the car ferry and France tomorrow morning. And then on to Madrid." Dorothy downs her pint in anticipation of the tray that has been set on the bar.

Pat hasn't taken her eyes off the young man.

"Medical supplies—expensive cargo. Does Dr. Bethune have support?" Shale continues her questioning of Dorothy.

"Not from the Canadian government, I'm sad to say. I don't know if Prime Minister King signed the Non-Intervention Treaty, but Hazen said First Secretary, Lester Pearson, told him at Canada House that the government is neutral. Bethune's undertaking will see no help from Mackenzie King."

Pat adds to Dorothy's account, "Remember—there is another fellow going with them. A Henning Sorenson, who represents the Committee to Aid Spanish Democracy."

Shale sits back to survey her friends. "An inspiring story."

Hazen arrives bearing gifts. Pat jumps up to clear away the empty glasses, while he unloads the tray. Hazen offers his hand to Dr. Clifden by way of introduction.

Alexandre and Sheila join the group as they all contemplate their drinks and the state of the world as filtered through the humane quest of three men.

Hazen engages the one person he has yet to speak with. "Dr. Clifden, it would seem that your efforts to bear witness to the ancients has been compromised by that upstart, Francisco Franco."

"Please, call me Shale. And yes, I would rather listen to the whispers of our ancestors, than the ravings of the world's egotists."

Sheila claps. "Well said. If only there was a hole big enough to drop them all in so that we can get on with the things that matter."

"Such as, Sheila?" Alexandre asks.

"Teaching children who have full bellies. Have you ever tried to have a meaningful conversation with a hungry adult, let alone a hungry child?" Sheila looks around the quiet table then reaches for her glass. "Altruism and starvation are not allies—not even among animals, who are much more fair-minded than we humans."

Dorothy sets her drink down and looks directly at Sheila. "Now I know what you were doing when you rode off into those brown and barren hills by yourself."

Sheila raises her head. "Becoming real. And those hills are far from barren. How else would I have learned?"

They all seem to be taking a breath until Shale turns her attention to Hazen. "Are we to understand that you are driving over the Pyrenees into Spain?"

"Yes, if the French haven't closed the border."

"Oh, we made our getaway over the Cantabrian Mountains to the Bay of Biscay." Pat seizes on mountains as an escape from the introspection around the table.

"Dr. Castro, have you driven the high passes of the border mountains?"

"Alexandre, please. And, no, the Pyrenees have been spared my skid marks."

"Oh, don't listen to him, Hazen. Those hairpin bends were no match for our driver. Not once did we fear for our lives, did we gang?" Pat beams, not expecting an answer.

"We've been out of touch, as you can well imagine, so I have no knowledge of the current state of Madrid." Alexandre focuses on

Hazen's destination. "When I left, the destruction was already heart-wrenching." He looks off through the window to the busy street. "The University of Madrid with all its collected knowledge . . . is there any of it that can be salvaged? I should be there to mount a recovery, to reclaim the light." His sudden laugh is as harsh as a bark. "Listen to me. What a fool I am to think it would be left untouched. Wisdom is dangerous. Every dictator knows that." Alexandre brings his gaze back to his companions, who, to him, appear shell-shocked.

Hazen nods, as if he's made up his mind. "I'll inquire for you. And when I get a chance, I'll send a telegram to Canada House."

Alexandre's respect for the young man is obvious on his face. Words seem superfluous, but are offered. "Thank you isn't enough, Hazen, nevertheless, thank you."

"We all do what we can to keep darkness at bay. I was only twelve years old when Germany signed the Armistice. Even as a boy growing up in Montreal, I knew what dark days the Great War brought."

Again, the quiet reflection around the Dray Horse's corner table.

"What's next?" Hazen asks.

Shale is quick to put forward one of her favourite places in London. "Foyles on Charing Cross Road."

"Of course, London wouldn't be London without an afternoon in the world's largest bookstore." Hazen is just a little surprised that Shale hadn't suggested Buckingham Palace. "There's a stop close by here—you can catch a Diddler."

They stare at their new friend without a thought to politeness.

"Oh, I see." Hazen chuckles. "An A1-class trolleybus. You know—double-decker, red."

೧೧೧೧

"There are people on the street reading books!" Pat climbs down from the trolleybus and claps her hands in delight. A man in a black bowler and overcoat engrossed in a tome is startled, losing his place in his book.

By the time he has found his page again, the SHE Gang and Alexandre are crossing the road to Foyles. There are long, low bookshelves on the sidewalk in front of the store windows, the shelves laden with books. Customers standing under the awnings are as intent as prospectors in a gold field.

Rather than elbow their way in under the awnings, the gang heads for the door, going straight to the mother lode. Overwhelmed, they simply stop in the main aisle to take it all in.

Shale is the first to speak. "Like I said—as many books as a library, but these ones you don't have to return."

Drawn by what speaks to them individually, they don't take long to go their separate ways.

After a time Alexandre and Shale meet among the science books.

"Are you just browsing?" Shale asks Alexandre.

"Browsing with a purpose. I've been watching for a book from the Oxford professor of philosophy, A. J. Ayer. He published an intriguing article in the journal, *Mind*. I had hoped it would lead to a book-length discourse."

"You are in luck, sir."

Alexandre and Shale turn to find a bespectacled man standing behind them.

"William Foyle. At your service."

"This is a pleasure. Your bookshop is my home away from home when I'm in London." Shale extends her hand.

"That is high praise."

"I am Dr. Clifden and this is my friend Dr. Castro."

"Well, Dr. Castro, Alfred Ayer's book, *Language, Truth, and Logic*, has just arrived. I have only two copies, you see, as it is a specialized topic."

"I hope they are not both spoken for. I would certainly like to take one away with me."

"Yes, of course, a volume is yours." William Foyle turns his attention to Shale. "And you, Dr. Clifden, is there something I can help you with?"

"Why, yes, I would like to know if it's true that when you heard the Nazis were burning books, you sent Adolf Hitler a telegram offering to buy his incendiary books."

A devilish smile crosses William Foyle's face. "It seemed a logical solution. I'm sure Alfred Ayer would agree." He reaches up to a shelf and hands Alexandre a newly minted copy of *Language, Truth, and Logic*.

"I don't suppose you heard back from Herr Hitler?" Shale asks.

"Oh, well, he's a busy man. Sadly, illusions of grandeur and world domination don't leave much time for correspondence."

Shale gives him a nod while Alexandre regards him cautiously before venturing a question of his own. "So, Mr. Foyle, you are of the opinion that war is on the horizon?"

"Don't let the Olympics in Berlin fool you. It was a show of power, nothing more. Hitler can't whitewash the fact that he has trampled the Treaty of Versailles by remilitarizing Western Germany. It's just a matter of time."

Shale shifts her gaze to a corner by the stairs leading to the second floor. "I noticed you have a stack of Hitler's *Mein Kampf*."

"Not for long. We're stuffing them in sandbags and stacking them on the roof to protect the store against air raids."

"As much as I consider books sacred objects, Mr. Foyle, you are my hero." Shale is genuine.

William Foyle gives them all fistfuls of bookmarks before they leave his kingdom.

⊙⊙⊙⊙

Another evening lecture at Canada House, the speaker this time is Northrop Frye, a young Canadian attending the University of Oxford. The Romantic English poet, William Blake, is obviously his passion. Frye introduces his audience to Blake's *Songs of Innocence and Experience* by suggesting that the poems are of the times, the current times, prophetic in the face of Nazism.

Hours later, the gang leaves Canada House quoting lines from Blake's poems to each other and Alexandre. By the time they have reached the Dray Horse Inn, their performance has become competitive: each trying to match Blake's verse to the headlines of the newspapers that lay discarded on their regular fireside table.

Sheila points to a *Times'* headline and challenges Dorothy. "What can you do with this? *Nazi Germany Passes New Law . . . Membership in the Hitler Youth Is Mandatory.*"

Dorothy examines the program given out at the Frye lecture and decides on lines from the Blake poem, *The Chimney Sweeper.* "*Because I was happy upon the heath, And smil'd among the winter's snow; They clothed me in the clothes of death, And taught me to sing the notes of woe.*"

The gang is loud in its praise. Loud enough to gather listeners.

Dorothy unfolds another paper and runs her finger down a column of print. "All right, back at you Sheila, *In Nazi Germany, the Death Penalty has been introduced for those who hoard their wealth abroad.*"

Sheila turns her glass slowly on the table, contemplating the changing light in the amber liquid and the lecture program before her. She chooses *The Human Abstract.* "*Pity would be no more, If we did not make somebody Poor; And Mercy no more could be, If all were as happy as we; And mutual fear brings peace, Till the selfish loves increase; Then Cruelty knits a snare, And spreads his bait with care.*"

Clapping from other tables around the pub breaks the silence. Those patrons standing at the bar venture closer to the fireplace and the gang's table.

Pat points to a headline and reads aloud, "*Five Thousand German Troops Landed at Cádiz in Spain to Fight for Franco.*" Pat looks up wide-eyed from the newspaper. Suddenly fully aware of the implications, she claps a hand over her mouth.

Shale diverts attention from the young woman. "*Tyger! Tyger! Burning bright In what deeps or skies Burnt the fire of thine eyes? What the hand, dare seize the fire?* Apologies to the poet." Shale places her hand beside Alexandre's where it is clenched in a fist on the table.

"Time for another round." Pat jumps up, scattering the onlookers who sense that something has changed.

ᏒᎧᏒᎧ

The hotel stairs register their now familiar protest as Shale descends to the lounge. She has managed to sleep to 4:11 a.m.—longer than usual.

Intent on opening the lounge door silently, she is startled by the smell of fresh cigarette smoke and the back of Alexandre's head. He sits on a high-backed sofa with newspapers spread around him. He seems to have taken a page from her book.

"Anything of interest?" She asks, making him start.

"Not interesting—alarming, chilling."

Shale recovers a paper tossed to the floor. "Oh, my, this *Times* is dated yesterday. How did you come by fresh newspapers?"

"I had Henry buy them for me." He turns a page and shakes out the fold in the paper.

"I see." Shale walks over to the bar and bends down to rifle through a pile of old newspapers kept on a shelf under the counter. She generally takes what she can find. This morning, the pile is diminished. It would seem the kitchen needed liners for their scrap pails. She digs out a *Sunday Times* from early November, only out of date by six weeks.

Sitting in a wingback chair across from Alexandre, Shale pages through her bounty. A headline snags her attention: *First Briton Killed In Spanish Civil War Remembered, Memorial Exhibition of Felicia Browne's Artworks*. "I don't believe it. A woman, an artist? Look at this, Alexandre." Shale thrusts the *Sunday Times* page at him.

He takes the paper reluctantly. "My God, her drawings, these faces—as sharp and hard as their weapons." He does not return the page; instead, he reads the whole article, quoting to Shale as he goes, "*Felicia Browne shot dead trying to blow up a Fascist munitions train. She was a member of the PSUC, the Cataluña Communist Militia.*"

When he finally looks up at Shale, his face is ashen. "Is this memorial exhibition still on?"

Shale checks the next page. "Yes, yes, it is. Until the new year."

"We must see it."

"Yes, we must."

Alexandre continues to read his papers closely. "We must also visit the All London Spanish Aid Council, the Women's Committee for Help to Spain, and the Spanish Medical Aid Committee."

"Why, Alexandre? Why would we visit these committees?"

"I want to know firsthand why they have chosen to involve themselves in Spanish affairs."

"Well, that's obvious."

"Not to me." They continue to read on, ostensibly ignoring each other.

After breakfast, the concierge standing in for Henry has two black cabs waiting for them at the hotel door. He has already given the drivers directions and paid the fares. Alexandre nods to him.

Over their morning coffee, Shale had related the story of Felicia Browne to the SHE Gang. They were astounded by Browne's audacity. Of course, they must honour her memory.

Alexandre and Shale occupy the first cab. The second cab, carrying the others, can barely contain the women's empathy.

"Such a shame. She was only thirty-two years old. Think of what she could have achieved with that kind of talent and bravery." Sheila is stunned.

"Yes, but think about what she did achieve in her short life. She put down political roots. I mean, really, after joining the British Communist Party, she travelled to Soviet Russia to see how it was done. To see how people lived and worked." Dorothy sounds almost wistful. As a member of the Young Communist League, she would not hesitate to follow in Felicia Browne's footsteps to Russia if given the chance.

"And then she went to Berlin to train as a stone mason and metal worker. Think of the sculpture she would have produced using those skills." Pat is sketching on the back of her program from the Canada House lecture.

The cabbie breaks their reveries. "We're here, ladies."

Shale and Alexandre are already in the gallery. The two of them stand reading a card attached to the wall beside a long glass display case.

The others gather around.

"I can't see. What does it say?" Sheila is at the back of the pack.

Shale reads aloud, "*On the twenty-fifth of August, in a failed attempt to dynamite a Fascist munitions train, Felicia Browne was fatally shot while assisting an injured Italian comrade. A sketchbook, retrieved from her possessions, was filled with drawings of her fellow fighters: these stoic men and women have been captured in Browne's lyrical, romantic, modernist style."*

Excitement has turned to awe and tears. Felicia Browne is larger than life. The gang hasn't been this quiet since entering Santa Cristina perched high in the Cantabrian Mountains.

They move along the display case. Gazing at the pages removed from her sketchbook, they are aware it was recovered in Spain and sent back to England, while her body was left where she fell. Her comrades were under fire and unable to mount a rescue.

Chastened, they turn from the display case to find a woman standing behind them. "Hello, I am Felicia's friend, Nan Youngman. Welcome. Do you have questions?"

"How did she come to be in Spain at this time?" Alexandre desires to understand Browne's intentions.

"Felicia and her friend Dr. Edith Bone were in Barcelona for the People's Olympiad. As left-wing artists, they were there to support the Soviet answer to Hitler's Olympics in Berlin."

"When was that?" Shale asks.

"Unfortunately, days before the rebellion against the Spanish Republic. They were strangers in a strange land when violence erupted in Barcelona on July nineteenth."

"It was early days—they could have fled." Alexandre is still perturbed.

"Apparently, not the way they had come. They had driven from France."

"Is that the only reason?" Alexandre probes deeper, his tone makes Nan Youngman uncomfortable.

"If you are implying that they were merely thrill seekers, then I suggest you speak to Felicia's close friend, Elizabeth Watson. She received letters from Felicia during this time." Nan turns and points to a door at the end of the gallery. "Elizabeth is in the studio."

The group dutifully walks away in the direction of Nan's outstretched arm.

Dorothy knocks gently on the door. "Come" is all she hears.

Elizabeth Watson is before an easel that supports a canvas containing an image of a curving bay with boats and naked bathers. "Yes?" she says, without taking her eyes off her work.

"Why did she stay?" Pat blurts out, arresting Elizabeth's attention.

She turns to survey them. "You must mean Felicia. It's simple really—Felicia Browne had principles and was a fighter."

"Is that enough?" Sheila asks. "Enough to risk your life?"

"I take it you saw the sketches of her fellow soldiers, the look in their eyes? Felicia possessed that kind of determination. She was resilient as well as having a knife-edge wit. But above all, she strove to give her life and art purpose." Elizabeth looks on expectant.

In a quiet voice Pat asks, "Did she come home?"

"No. If lucky, she is in a mass grave rather than scavenged by birds and dogs." Elizabeth turns back to her painting. "Thank you for caring enough to ask."

Once outside the gallery, they stop to get their bearings and decide they can walk to Canada House. It is a solemn advance along the streets and across Trafalgar Square.

Waiting at Canada House are cablegrams for Dorothy, Pat, and Sheila. Nothing for Alexandre from Hazen Sise. Envelopes in hand, food and drink call to them from the Dray Horse Inn.

After placing their orders with the barmaid, they settle in, using the table knives to open their envelopes.

Dorothy is the first to speak. "My God, she's done it again."

"Who? What?" Shale is first with the salient questions.

"Oh, sorry. My friend, childhood friend is the queen of the unexpected. My father has written to say that Gina, now Jean Watts, is going to Spain to report for the *Daily Clarion*. He suspects she will try to enlist in the International Brigades."

"What is the *Daily Clarion*?" Alexandre asks.

"The Canadian Communist newspaper. She must have beat out a few fellows I know for that job." Dorothy is shaking her head, obviously amused.

"Why does your friend have two names?" Pat is more concerned about particulars.

"She's a chameleon with four names, actually. The two she was christened with—Myrtle Eugenia and the two we gave her at school— Gina and Jean. Jeanie was our fearless leader, the voice of resistance against authority."

"It would seem nothing has changed," Sheila suggests with a

note of respect in her voice.

"What you must also understand is that Jean was born a poet. By way of example, when we were just girls, I teased her about leaning out her bedroom window every Monday morning to say hello to the garbagemen."

Their lunch arrives from the kitchen and Alexandre retrieves the drinks from the bar.

"And—" Pat is impatient, displeased by the interruption.

Dorothy looks up from her plate, a wry smile on her face. "And what Jean said was *They have the greatest way of talking back and joking. They make words exciting—honestly, Dee.*"

"I would say that as a girl, she was already learning to be one of the boys." Shale winks at Dorothy. "Your friend will find a place for herself in Spain."

Alexandre studies Shale, realizing that he knows very little about the psychology of girls and women.

From her place beside Dorothy, Pat can see there is more to Mr. Livesay's cablegram. "Your father has sent you a long flimsy. What else does it say?"

"Flimsy?" Sheila is baffled.

"Nothing flimsy about J.F.B. Livesay. But no, 'flimsy' is what the English call a telegram. And, yes, there is more. My father has requested I write an article about my time in Spain. He will see it is published in the Canadian newspapers." Dorothy looks straight at Alexandre. Of course, it would mean the House of Castro would be exposed. Her kidnapping and maltreatment in Galicia revealed to the public.

Her gaze does not go unnoticed.

"Well, I received a flimsy flimsy," Sheila says. "Typical of my mother—*Come home now*. Short and sweet."

"Me, too." Pat sounds indignant. "But not typical of my father, who told me life is a great adventure, a great game, but always stick to your ideals. Now he's telling me to go stay with my Aunt Bibbi, where I'll be safe."

"You have family in London?" Shale is astounded by this news.

"Well, not exactly—Purley near Croydon, on the outskirts of London."

Sheila pushes back her chair. "More drinks?"

The table falls silent; the only thing left to do is concentrate on their plates.

When Sheila returns, she brings a newspaper with her. "Look at this headline, *Mussolini Agrees to Send Troops to Spain*." She reads on, "*The Corpo di Truppe Volontarie will arrive in late December to aid Franco*."

Shale looks to Alexandre. "This morning in the lounge, did you read about this move by Mussolini?"

"Yes. And it's time we made a visit to the Spanish Medical Aid Committee, and the Spanish Women's Committee for Help to Spain." Alexandre sounds beleaguered.

"To what end, Alexandre?" Dorothy is gentle. She will not write an article on Spain for her father. At least not yet.

"To gauge what can be done for Spain. What is being done," is his short answer.

Shale realizes Alexandre is looking forward—a place the rest of them have not come to yet. "Yes, at least we can go and thank them for their efforts."

They step out through the public house doors and come face-to- face with two huge dark heads. As they approach the massive dray horses, Pat quips, "Our cab awaits."

Shale goes to speak to the driver, who sits well above the wagon box, which holds four barrels of ale. Dressed in black, including bowler, he is perched on what must be a six-foot high metal frame with padded seat. Both Shale and Alexandre must crane their necks.

Having asked permission, the gang gathers to admire the muscled horses, shiny black with brushing. Their white, feathered fetlocks are soft coverings for massive hooves. The giants seem to be pleased to have their noses stroked.

Alexandre leads the way back to Trafalgar Square and approaches the cabbies talking and smoking around the cab rank. He hires two cabs and gives the drivers the address for the Office of the Spanish Women's Committee for Help to Spain. The group splits up as it did in the morning, and once Shale and Alexandre are on their way, Shale asks, "How did you get the address for this organization?"

"Henry has been very helpful. He also supplied the address

for the Spanish Medical Aid Committee. We'll visit them as well."

"Are these committees the work of expatriate Spanish women and doctors as the names suggest?"

"No, I don't believe so. These are British initiatives. From what I've read and confirmed with Henry's assistance, there are at least ten such organizations."

Shale can understand his gratitude for the help to his homeland, but rather than appreciation, she feels fear. The British are organizing because they see beyond Spain to war on the horizon.

♋♋♋

They are seated in a high-ceilinged room, all oak panelling and red leather. Simpson's in the Strand dates from 1828 and began its illustrious gastronomic career as one of London's celebrated chess rooms.

Simpson's had been Pat's suggestion for supper after a gruelling day. All wrung out was how she described her emotional state. A hardy English meal would put her right. This meant roast beef, gravy, and Yorkshire pudding, rounded out with a selection of humble vegetables. Drinks first, of course, drinks and talk.

Dorothy's expression is creating deep frown lines. "I can't help but feel our efforts in Canada are just child's play." She takes a notebook from her handbag. "Besides the two offices we visited today, here is a list of the other aid organizations."

"Awe, no, Dorothy. Can't we just sit back and relax. That's why I suggested Simpson's."

"Just bear with me." Dorothy's political ardour is apparent. She starts down her list. "Women's International League for Peace and Freedom, Artists International Association, Basque Children's Committee, Women's Co-operative Guild, All London Spanish Aid Council—"

"Fascism is very real to the British," Shale redirects the onslaught. "A common anti-fascist slogan here is 'Fascism spreads terror; keep it out.'"

Suddenly, Alexandre pushes back his cardinal red chair and

walks away. Shale calls to him, but he just shakes his head. She follows as far as the dining room entrance. He leaves through the main door to the street.

Sheila is at Shale's side. "Let him go. Walking along the river will do him good. Come on, some food and drink will do you good."

Shale and Sheila arrive back at the table to find a silver-domed carving trolley awaiting their return. Once seated, the waiter reveals a rib roast of Scottish beef along with an impressive carving knife. The brandishing of a knife and the smell of food captures their attention.

The gang forsakes dessert listed under "Pudding" on the menu for cocktails.

☙☙☙

The hotel's breakfast room is deserted. The SHE Gang arrived back to the hotel late last night and rather tipsy. The waitress is now cleaning up and not best pleased to see the latecomers. She directs them to a table that she has laid for the lunch service.

"We don't mean to inconvenience the kitchen, but would it be too much to request coffee, toast and hardboiled eggs all around?" The waitress heeds Shale, since she does not appear to be hung-over. Shale receives a curt nod for her efforts.

"And why are you looking so fresh?" Sheila demands.

"Experience—not much to do in the evenings on a dig site. My women colleagues can out party the men."

The waitress returns with a carafe of coffee and a note. She hands the envelope to Shale, then works her way around the table filling cups.

Shale opens the missive with a butter knife and slips out a piece of hotel stationary. A glance reveals it is from Alexandre. She reads it to the others, "*Gone to my agent's office. Meet you for lunch at the Dray Horse.*"

"Well, he's sure being enigmatic. What's got into him?" Dorothy asks.

"Largesse. You saw him at the aid offices. All the questions he asked." Sheila surveys the table. "I think he was stunned to hear about the kind of fundraising it takes to send medical workers, ambulances, and equipment to Spain. And the women's cooperatives, making clothing to contribute, while they also support 144 Basque children. And the list goes on."

"Alexandre is as aware as we are that this is not a time of plenty in Britain," Pat adds. "I mean—look at what the Women's Committee for Help to Spain has done organizing work parties to make clothing. These parties are made up of unemployed women working in disused factories."

"But 'largesse'? Alexandre is humbled by their efforts on behalf of Spain? Or is he shamed?" Dorothy typically goes to the heart of the matter.

"Only he can answer those questions. Best over a pint or two in the Dray Horse. In the meantime, I thought we might take in some culture." The SHE Gang must wait to hear Shale's proposal. Breakfast trays have arrived.

♋♋♋

The Ionic columns of the British Museum succeed in making the women feel small as they climb the stairs to the entrance. With the enormous wealth of human history housed within those walls, they decide the best approach is just to wander from hall to hall. Not set on understanding the quote from Alexander Pope, '*The glory, jest and riddle of the world*,' painted in gold above a huge door: they simply drink it in.

Released from duties as their guide, Shale is free to indulge her fascination for the Egyptian *Book of the Dead*. The Papyrus of Ani rests in the British Museum rather than in Ani's sarcophagus. The remnants of this papyrus scroll from 1250 BC beguile the eye with images both coloured and hieroglyphic. Images meant to help the dead into the afterlife through magic spells. Shale is hunting among the fragments for Anubis, the jackal-headed god who weighs the hearts of the dead against a feather.

Reunited, they all agree the morning has passed too quickly

as they leave the forest of Ionic columns for the snug burrow of the pub.

Alexandre has arrived ahead of them. He stares into the flames of the fireplace seemingly unaware of their arrival. They join him, glad for the warmth; after all, it is December. Not a Canadian winter, but winter nevertheless.

Yet another telegram lies in front of him on the table, next to his untouched pint.

"News?" Shale asks.

"From Hazen Sise. They made it to Madrid."

"And?"

"I am going back to Spain. My agent is finding me passage on a ship."

The women have yet to sit down.

"Why?" Pat is strangely aware that all the questions so far are single words.

"Franco is mounting a campaign against Madrid—to cut it off from the rest of the Republican territory." Alexandre pushes the flimsy toward Shale. "If I'm going to recover the University's Research Archives, it has to be now."

After a long period of silence, the SHE Gang finally sits down at the table.

"I'm coming with you." Dorothy holds up a hand to pre-empt dissent. "I'll help you. More hands make short work. Then I'll go find Jean Watts."

"I have hands, and like my father said, I have ideals to standby, to fight for if necessary." Pat is not defiant; she is resolute.

"More hands?" Shale is looking at Sheila, whose eyes are down studying her hands.

"As long as you can put a rifle in mine, I'll guard your backs," is Sheila's answer.

"I'll drink to that, when I get one." Shale turns to the bar.

"No." Alexandre is emphatic. "I will not endanger you."

"Not your choice to make." Shale looks him in the eyes. "And don't say you won't help us secure transportation because we are capable of finding our own way."

Alexandre shakes his head.

" I want to know what has become of the University's collection of Prehistoric artifacts. They may need rescuing as well."

While drinks and food are ordered, Alexandre stares into the flames of the fireplace. Finally he shifts his attention to the women. He appears to be studying them. "I have conducted research into the principles of friendship, and the four of you break with all the norms. Your friendship is an aberration based on compassion not envy. Compassion destroys conceit. And in knowing that, I trust your motives. But if something were to happen to you—" Alexandre cannot finish the sentence. He is up and gone before they can allay his fears.

Shale regards the others. "With or without him, if this is what you truly want, we will find a way."

After lunch, Shale commandeers the hotel telephone. She calls the Smithsonian to consult with Dr. Abbot. And yes, he will contact the museum directors in Spain, if they are to be found. As with Shale, he is keen to know how Spain is managing to keep its cultural treasures safe.

෨෨෨

Alexandre has disappeared on some mission of his own. They have not seen him for three days, although, according to concierge Henry, Dr. Castro is still registered at the hotel.

The women have a quest of their own that has them spending days in the Canada House Reading Room, scouring the newspapers, both British and international. Dorothy is their in-house translator for the French and Spanish papers, while Sheila takes on the German. They want to know what they will be up against if they return to Spain. What they find is Spain inked with the politics of Europe.

Dorothy suggests that in order to get firsthand accounts, she will telephone her father and have him send her the dispatches he has received from The Canadian Press reporters in Spain, especially Madrid.

With this in mind, Dorothy finds the secretary to the High

Commissioner, Mike Pearson, in his office. She knows he has a direct line to her father in The Canadian Press office in Toronto.

Of course, her father wants to know the reason for her request. She dodges the question for the moment by explaining that the news is for her Spanish friend Dr. Castro. Sounding unconvinced, he tells her that she can collect the reports from the London Bureau of The Canadian Press. He will give the manager permission to release them to her.

ᏩᏩᏩ

Breakfast without Alexandre again. The SHE Gang has given up trying to fathom what has become of him. Their best guess: he has been seduced and is now a love slave.

They are still giggling at this scenario when Henry approaches the table with a letter for Shale. She reaches for the butter knife.

"Well, what is it? Is it private?" Pat is impatient.

"If you must know, it's an invitation to dine at Simpson's."

"Oh, so you have a secret admirer . . . do tell."

"No secrets among us. Alexandre has invited one and all. Dinner is by way of an apology for his absence this week."

"Perhaps we'll get an explanation between our beef and pudding." Dorothy would prefer answers to trifle.

"Couldn't be better." Sheila has their attention. "We'll have time to collect the dispatches from The Canadian Press Bureau, and have a private read and confab at Canada House. If we agree to go back to Spain, we're going to need Mike Pearson's help."

With Henry's directions in hand, it doesn't take them long to find the Bureau. A call from J.F.B. Livesay has produced a manila envelope ready and waiting at reception—so far so good. They're hoping the Reading Room will be free of readers when they arrive.

In luck again, they occupy a quiet corner, and Dorothy hands around the pages. They are horrified by what they discover in the reports. As they read, their quiet corner becomes silent as if they have forgotten to breathe.

"Let me read you what Fredrick Griffin wrote for the *Daily Star*,

"Madrid is defended by a seemingly impregnable series of trenches and wide stone breastworks. Every street is tremendously barricaded, but the enigma is the quality of the untrained and untested, highly individualistic citizen defenders when placed under intensive barrage. On the Spanish character, rather than on her arms, hangs the fate of Madrid and Spain during the coming days and weeks.

Madrid awaits its fate stoically, its million people existing day to day. Today, in the rain, I walked again from the Gran Vía past the barricades into Blasco Ibanez St., through part of the terribly devastated west fringe of the city. The rain and mud made the torn up streets and ravaged homes and buildings the acme of desolation. There were wide, shattered, deserted vistas, yet washing hung to dry in sheltered spots among the ruins and scores of women might be seen carrying bundles, evidently busy at the never-ending work of retrieving things of value."
Dorothy takes a long breath. "Griffin sees the people, so should we."

Sheila looks down at her pages. "The worst fighting is at the University City campus and the Clinical Hospital at the School of Medicine." She looks up at Shale.

"Here's something." Pat is disturbed by what she is hearing from the others. "A group formed to protect Spain's art—the Committee for Artistic Treasures During the Civil War. They're working to fortify museums, to collect public and private art, catalogue it, and move thousands of artworks out of Madrid."

Shale looks at the women, her friends, each sitting in a nest of papers. "We must carve out niches for ourselves."

"Such as?" Dorothy has some ideas of her own.

"Well, I think Pat has found a committee she can work for. I'm sure they could use help with all the documents they are creating."

"Fine. What about me?" Sheila asks.

It is Dorothy who provides an answer. "I'm going to ask my father to make you a reporter. As a woman, you would bring a unique perspective, especially since there seems to be a women's militia."

"Why not you?" Sheila counters.

"Nepotism for one thing. Employing family is frowned upon. That said, I'm an academic who knows her way around research. My skills and the fact that I read Spanish make me of use at the University of Madrid."

"What about the article for your father?" Pat asks.

'Oh, that would be a travel piece by a Canadian citizen abroad. No payment involved."

"So, it looks like we have work to do," Shale declares with something like pride in her voice.

"Beginning with my father and Mike Pearson. In both cases, I think we have our work cut out for us." Dorothy is looking determined.

☾☽☾☽

The elusive Alexandre is seated in Simpson's dining room when they arrive. The women examine him closely as they take their places around the table.

"Hello, stranger." Shale is the first to address him.

"Speaking of strange." Alexandre gazes from one to the other. "Strangely beautiful. It's as if my dining companions have walked out of the fashion pages. What wonderful dresses and so right for each of you."

"Right? Please explain." Dorothy is quizzical.

"Well, Miss Livesay— navy blue and white, dark and light; dot and dash pattern, literary; high collar, queenly."

"Who would have guessed—a psychologist and a poet," is her ironic reply.

"And what of my dress?" Pat is quick to ask.

"Buttons and bows, full skirt—decidedly feminine."

"What of the colour?"

"Pink suits your dark hair."

Pat is obviously pleased.

Alexandre surveys the table, looking for assent to continue. Shale and Sheila remain noncommittal.

"What of the others?" Pat demands. "You're not finished. It wouldn't be fair."

"If you say so. Well, Sheila is in goddess green, reaffirming her connection with Mother Earth. While Shale, in brown and beige stripes, is one with her caves. The double row of brass buttons down the front of her matching jacket suggests the discipline of a professional."

The ladies are astounded by Alexandre's performance.

"What did you just do?" Sheila is bewildered.

"More to the point: how did you do it?" Dorothy insists.

"Symbolism. We are unconsciously attracted to those things in our world that reflect our inner selves." He turns to Sheila. "Your friend Rorschach understands this principle, as does Shale in her analysis of cave art." Alexandre waits for a response. When none is forthcoming, he returns them to the obvious: "Shall we dine."

Wine arrives. The wine steward seems more attentive than usual, Pat observes. It's apparent their fashionable new frocks have made an impression, aided by the sleek hats and matching shoes and handbags.

Shale raises her wine glass. "To Spain!"

Alexandre is taken by surprise. He covers by raising his glass as well.

"You have news, Alexandre?" Shale's toast has opened the subject.

"Yes, of course, my absence. I have been engaged with the Spanish Medical Aid Committee, specifically the treasurer, Lady Hastings. To get to the meat of the matter before our Scottish beef arrives: together we have purchased an ambulance and filled it with medical supplies. I leave for Spain presently."

Their silence is pronounced, magnifying the clatter of cutlery on china.

"Well, I hope your vehicle is large enough for four passengers." Shale is aware of the consternation writ large on Alexandre's face. "We have work to do in Spain."

"You're not soldiers, doctors, fire wardens—Madrid is a battleground."

"Yes, we know—we've read the latest news coming out of Madrid. And we know where we are needed."

Alexandre is about to protest when the carving trolley arrives at their table.

Once their plates are full, Shale resumes, "Sheila has been hired by Mr. Livesay to report from Madrid on behalf of The Canadian Press. Pat has volunteered her serves to the Committee for Artistic

Treasures During the Civil War—Dr. Abbot has contacted the Prado on her behalf. Dorothy and I have the tacit approval of the Canadian High Commissioner to mount a rescue of valuable knowledge and artifacts from the University. We will help you with the archives. And, yes, we have read the reports on the fighting at University City."

The party of handsome women and one sullen man concentrate on their plates.

The atmosphere in the gilded room is tense. Alexandre is distracted and the SHE Gang assumes he is pondering reasons why they cannot accompany him. Before he can raise his objections, Pat suggests they forego dessert in favour of the cocktail bar in Florin Court. The bartender has a unique skill, and the pianist plays Cole Porter songs.

The cab drops them at the door of an undulating building. The nine storeys of honey-coloured brick and glass pay homage to the Art Deco passion for curving lines. A stunning apartment block, it boasts a roof garden, swimming pool, public restaurant, and bar. The first time Pat walked up the curved stairs to the entrance on the arm of a cousin, she vowed one day she would have a Florin Court flat.

The porter directs them to a set of serpentine stairs wrapped with a banister of black wrought iron. They descend and approach a set of dark doors with porthole windows. Inside the bar, light streams off of steel and glass. The walls are covered with metal screens bearing cut-out patterns that would make an Egyptian pharaoh proud. The room is furnished with salmon pink leather chairs, moss green velvet sofas, and metal tables in brushed gold.

"We've stumbled into someone's boudoir" is Dorothy's assessment.

They laugh as they find a table large enough for their mob.

"Shall we order? What do you recommend, Pat?" Sheila is eyeing the bar, where many of the patrons sit on high stools.

"Not for me to say." Pat is looking suspiciously coy.

"Pardon?"

"Wait and see," is all she will reveal.

The bartender leaves his post behind the bar to join them at their golden table. After a cursory welcome, he stands and studies each of them closely.

Finally, he produces a small leather-bound notebook and a stylish pen. "For the lady in green, a Robin Hood; for the lady in pink, a Marie Antoinette; for the lady in navy and white, a Bluebeard; for the lady in brown, a T.E. Lawrence of Arabia; and for the gentleman, a Don Quixote"

They are spellbound. The barman closes his book, bows, and leaves.

"How could I possibly have explained that to you?" Pat's gaze follows the departing man with wide-eyed admiration.

"Do you think he knows that T.E. Lawrence was an archaeologist?" Shale asks.

"I didn't know that," Sheila confesses.

"Who is Bluebeard?" Alexandre thinks he sounds preferable to Cervantes' knight-errant.

"A wealthy man who perpetually marries and murders each wife," Dorothy offers.

"Oh, I see." Alexandre reclaims *The Ingenious Gentleman Don Quixote of La Mancha*.

"'Bluebeard' is a French folktale. As to the connection?" Dorothy shrugs. "The colour blue, I suppose." She glances at Alexandre. "I prefer your earlier flight of fancy to the barman's."

The pianist arrives before the cocktails, and opens the evening with Cole Porter's *Anything Goes*.

A young man approaches their table. "May I leave my drink on your table?" He directs his query to Pat.

She nods.

He finishes his request: "While we dance." He holds out his hand.

Pat glances at his hand and then at her gang, cocks her head, and says, "Why not."

They smile at the tall young woman in a pink dress with the short young man in a white dinner jacket.

Alexandre watches the watchers—the young man's friends standing at the bar. They consult and make their move. They edge around the dance floor as they home in on the golden table. Unlike their dancing friend, the best they can do for openers is to introduce themselves. Alexandre lets them stand and shuffle awhile before inviting them to join the table. They are quick to find chairs.

The piano player has changed the tempo, introducing a softer mood with Kern and Fields's *The Way You Look Tonight*. Alexandre turns to Shale. "Would you care to dance, Dr. Clifden?"

"Why, Dr. Castro, how nice of you to ask."

They join Pat and her admirer on the starburst dance floor. "I'm sure you noticed."

"Ah, yes, Dr. Castro. I'm sure those young men are wondering just what kind of nest of educated vipers they've stumbled on."

"Dorothy will straighten them out." He chuckles.

He swallows his words almost immediately as Dorothy leads the least gawky of the interlopers to the dance floor.

Just before closing time, Alexandre announces to the table that they leave for Spain the next morning.

Their new friends refuse to let them go without an explanation. The cleaners push them out of the bar, so they take over the lobby. When they part company, the lads have gone from boisterous to thoughtful. This will be a story they readily tell.

What Alexandre fails to point out at 3:00 a.m. is that the next day is not the one dawning.

Over one final lunch at the Dray Horse, he lays out the plan. Essentially they will follow the tire tracks of Sise and Bethune. But first, Alexandre will accompany them to Canada House to meet with Mike Pearson. Alexandre wants personal assurance that the young women have notified their families and have the support of the High Commissioner. He will make it clear that this is a humanitarian endeavour and Canada should have their backs. The card up his sleeve: Lady Hastings and the President of the Spanish Medical Aid Committee, Dr. Christopher Addison, MP, have made calls this morning to Mike Pearson's boss.

☙❧

France slides away under their wheels. They've made good time despite the need to stop and stretch their legs frequently; the wood-panelled station wagon is cramped. Alexandre has decided they will spend the night in Paris. They all need some proper rest before making the long journey to Bordeaux, where the home of his colleague is to be their staging ground for tackling the Pyrenees. What he has not revealed to the ladies is that he has asked his friend Felipe to acquire a small arsenal of handguns. No hardship for Felipe, who has been a gun collector since his stint in a military academy as a youth. He is also willing to teach Alexandre's companions some basic skills.

Paris welcomes them with a sunset. Alexandre knows the City of Light well and heads for the hotel he believes to be the only place in the capital a Spaniard can properly lay his head. The Hotel Majestic was once Palacio Castilla, home in exile to Queen Isabella the Second of Spain.

After checking in, Alexandre joins the ladies standing in the lobby. "Dinner at eight. It was recommended I make reservations."

The women look as if a stranger has just accosted them.

"We have nothing to wear." Pat is aghast.

"We packed our knapsacks with our work clothes. We're going to a war, not a cotillion." Shale looks around her at the ornate lobby and shakes her head.

"A what?" Pat asks.

"A formal soirée," Dorothy explains.

Alexandre consults his wristwatch. "We're going shopping."

"Just so we can dine at the Majestic? This is frivolous." Dorothy is decidedly unimpressed.

"Perhaps I should have given you a fuller picture before we left London and those lovely cocktail dresses behind. In Madrid, you will be meeting people in high-level positions. They will expect you to be attired as the professional women you are. So, no, this is not about Palacio Castilla; it's about making an impression in Madrid." He holds up his hand as Dorothy prepares to speak. "Yes, the city is under siege. Soon, it will be an all-out battlefield. But in order to do the work we have taken on, we will need help from people in authority."

"Well, Parisian fashion should make an impression." Shale turns to the door.

"One small problem." Sheila lifts her shoulders in a gesture of futility. "Money."

"Not a problem," Alexandre says briskly. "I'm buying. I need to spend the money the Smithsonian paid for the Castro Collection before my brother comes looking for it."

"In that case, lead on." Pat hums *Anything Goes* as they leave the hotel.

༄༄༄

At the crest of a hill, Alexandre pulls the station wagon off the road onto a small patch of hard-packed earth. Below them a valley stretches away filled with row upon row of vines reaching tendrils to the sky. Menacing clouds cover the sun, frustrating the search for life giving light. Among the vineyards, there are whitewashed stone houses, with the exception of one that has a touch of the Mediterranean in the Grecian blue of its window frames and doors.

Alexandre smiles to himself, certain that this is his friend's tribute to Iberia and the South. Here they are, Felipe and Veva, tucked away two hours southeast of Bordeaux, the closest village being tiny Saint Ferme—the world must seem very far away. It is idyllic, and yet there are signs of unrest: for one, their progress from Paris slowed by trucks packed with soldiers heading south to the border with Spain. A flash of guilt galvanizes Alexandre, as lightning sears the sky. His presence will be an unwelcome reminder of what his friends escaped.

As Alexandre drives into the yard, two robust Pyrenean mountain dogs greet them. He rolls down the window. "Peli, Digna. Soy yo."

The great shaggy beasts stop in their tracks, and then charge the car, jumping at the window to lick Alexandre's face. He laughs as he holds their big heads in his hands.

Alexandre leaves the station wagon and walks toward the house. He doesn't get far before two young girls lay claim to a leg each like limpets. The only way to unfasten them is to promise a carousel swing. Holding one at a time by the arms, he lifts the girl and twirls in a circle.

A man and a woman approach, each carrying a toddler. Alexandre's friend and colleague shifts the child to one arm and throws the other around Alexandre's neck. They press foreheads until the child begins to squirm.

Alexandre engulfs mother and child. All is still until the girls realize there are others in the station wagon. They open the doors and attempt to clamour in. There is no room. The women get out into the warmth of a southern sun. The girls take Pat's and Sheila's hands, leading them toward the house. "Our new SHE Gang," Pat exclaims. Shale and Dorothy join them by each taking a child's free hand.

Introductions include passing around toddlers for cooing hugs. Veva rescues both boys and directs Felipe to settle their guests into their rooms.

The SHE Gang and Alexandre return to the station wagon to retrieve their suitcases and knapsacks. Of course, the girls are right there to help and inspect.

Felipe takes them to a flight of stairs leading down from the main entrance. "The staircase is narrow: you'll need to carry your luggage in front of you. Those are sturdy suitcases," he remarks."

"They'll come in handy," Alexandre says.

With each step the air cools by subterranean degrees. Bare-armed, the women shiver.

Felipe notices their goose flesh. "Veva has laid out woolen robes for you, to ward off the chill down here."

Four bedrooms, two to a side off a hallway, show signs of being newly made.

Alexandre stops to contemplate the four doors. "So, you and Veva are preparing for more children?"

Felipe turns to Alexandre. "We rather hoped you were coming to live with us. You and a wife, perhaps." He raises an eyebrow that only Alexandre can see. "Instead, you bring us four lovely ladies."

Pat is first off the mark. "Sheila and I can share this big room at the end."

The others stake their claims and begin unpacking the necessities, but that is not enough for Mecha and Paz. The girls wander from room to room, opening suitcases, lifting out dresses, blouses, skirts and jackets.

"Tags? These clothes still have the shop tags. Why?" Mecha asks Pat.

"We bought them in Paris just before leaving to come here."

"And the suitcases to put them in," Sheila adds.

"Such beautiful clothes." Paz lifts a magenta blouse to her face. "Ah, silk."

"What do you know about silk?" Pat asks, surprised by the young girl.

"I know I love it. Maman's wedding dress is silk. It is kept in a special wooden box, a cedar box."

"I like this wool jacket with the cape attached. Very fashionable, although I wouldn't have chosen black," Mecha pronounces.

Pat and Sheila are astounded by the mature sensibilities of these girls.

"Let's go see what Uncle Xandre has in his suitcase. Maybe he brought us dollies." Paz takes Mecha's hand as they leave swiftly, driven by the thought of gifts.

The lovely ladies hang up their new, fashionable clothes to release the wrinkles. There are long skirts and fitted jackets, elegantly appointed with wide lapels accented by lines of topstitching and trim; long slim belted dresses with large contrasting collars, or velvet inset at the shoulders, or side-pleats softening the lines of the skirt; and warm winter coats, all of which are black in colour.

As the women gather in the hall, they are startled by screams coming from Alexandre's room. The girls bolt down the hallway waving what look like bright flags. On closer scrutiny, it appears Uncle Xandre has brought the girls kites not dollies. The SHE Gang approves.

Veva is in the kitchen at one end of the long, open room. The women are helping her make dinner. While at the other end of the room, the men mind the children. The noise meets in the middle over the heavy homemade table.

Mecha and Paz clatter about setting the table. Their labours are punctuated by screams from the twin boys riding Alexandre's bouncing knees—a couple of chubby vaqueros.

The meal is joyous chaos, the children vying for the attention of the adults, especially the guests. Felipe suggests they walk among the vineyards as far as the barn, once the children are put to bed. It is a peace offering, peace and quiet to come.

The sun has set, and to balance the heavens, the full moon has risen. The earth exhales, the scent of hot soil and green sweat. The vines cast lace shadows at their feet. No one speaks. They are remembering themselves—the selves that London and Paris abducted.

"Do you walk among the vines at night, when the work is done?" Sheila asks her hosts.

"Yes, most nights. How did you know?" Veva sounds bemused.

"The dogs, Digna and Peli, automatically took up their posts outside the children's bedrooms.

"You're very observant," Felipe remarks.

"Animals reveal much more than humans. That, and I'm honing my skills for Spain."

"How so?" Felipe looks at Alexandre, then back at Sheila.

"I'm a newly appointed reporter for The Canadian Press."

Felipe studies the young woman. Before he can respond, Veva steps out of the shadows. "You're going to bear witness to this atrocity, aren't you? Aren't you all?"

The silence is country deep. When the shock subsides, Shale speaks. "Spain is the future. The testing ground for spreading Fascism by force. The world cannot afford to turn away. We must oblige people to look."

And look they do. The whole group stares at Shale.

Finally, Alexandre asks, "Have you understood this all along?"

"Yes, as an archaeologist, I bear witness to our past. I preserve who we were. As a human being, I am tasked with preserving our humanity. Franco, Mussolini, Hitler are thieves of the worst kind. They would steal our progress, what we have become—compassionate creatures."

The voiceless dark is torn by sharp barks coming from the house. All eyes turn to the sound.

"Digna telling us that Paz is sleepwalking. Our daughter has a nighttime life."

They move down the path quickly. Felipe cautions them, "Don't hurry, you might sprain an ankle in the dark. Digna will see that Paz comes to no harm."

Child and dog are sitting side by side at the edge of a still pond. Digna's tail thumps the ground, telegraphing their whereabouts.

Felipe gathers Paz into his arms while Digna licks his face. "Home to bed for all of us, I think."

❧❧❧

The next morning, Felipe and his guests assemble in the barn. He shows them the wooden gathering baskets, the wooden grape scoops, the wooden box screens, a mobile grape press on a rough built wooden wheelbarrow, and the large wooden barrel presses. There is no sign, no smell of winemaking.

Felipe explains that they take their grapes to their neighbour, who is teaching him and Veva how to make wine the traditional way.

"You have made a good life for yourself, my friend." Alexandre appears almost sad.

"And so could you. All I can think about is how to convince you not to go back to Spain, Xandre. I want you to be here, on this earth, to see your godson and namesake grow to manhood."

The women look on, torn apart by the scene.

Felipe pauses, turmoil apparent on his face. He moves to one of the large barrel presses, steps up on the short ladder attached to the side, and reaches, bent double, inside.

He comes down the stairs, holding a burlap sack closed at the top with a drawstring. "I've set up a shooting range out in the back, come along."

Felipe opens the burlap bag and places five pistols on a long bench. He has stretched a pillowcase between two saplings at the edge of a grove. The target painted on the linen is blue, the same as the trim on the house.

"These are German made Mauser C96 semi-automatic pistols— Bolo for short. Favoured by the Bolsheviks. Xandre, you remember this gun, don't you?"

"Of course, I remember all your guns, Felipe. Always wise to know where there's a ready arsenal."

"Anyone else familiar with firearms?"

"Rifle—hunting rifle," Sheila offers.

"My father is a soldier. He's given me a few lessons," Pat reveals.

"My friend Jean Watts had a BB gun when we were kids. We plunked at cans and beer bottles." The memory makes Dorothy smile.

"I've heard Canada is a wild place, but what of America?" Felipe turns to Shale, who is examining the Mausers closely.

"Gangsters. America has gangs. Lots of guns, lots of blood."

"And yourself?" Alexandre is assessing risk.

"As a field archaeologist, I'm required to trained in self-defence, including firearms."

"Well, let me introduce you, hands-on, to the unloaded Bolo. Each of you pick-up a pistol. Feel the weight. Try the wooden grip. Point at the target, test the front sight and pull the trigger. Just get used to it. It's got a ninety-nine-millimetre barrel. It's chambered for the standard 7.63 by 25 mm Mauser. The magazine is the box in front of the trigger." Felipe pauses allowing them to catch up. "Now load the box magazine with cartridges, and we'll do some target practice. Xandre will show you how to load."

The morning passes quickly but not quietly as they become familiar with the pistols and Felipe coaches them on sight alignment, trigger control, single-hand and double-hand placement. He warns them, "The cartridge cases eject out of the top of the magazine into your line of sight; as well, the recoil may cause you to lift the barrel, so keep your eyes on the front sight."

Shale asks Felipe how Veva feels about him using her bed linen for target practice.

"She is happy to sacrifice it for Xandre," is his response.

"I will repay her, of course." Alexandre smiles.

Felipe sets his sights on Xandre. "You can repay Veva by coming back alive."

6

WITNESS

Madrid, Huete,Villanueva de la
Jara, Valencia

6

WITNESS

Madrid is dark. Their headlights pick out hollow buildings standing in gardens of rubble.

"We would be lost," Alexandre mutters.

Shale is beside him in the front seat. "What is it, Alexandre?"

"Oh, if I didn't know this city so well—no landmarks, no street signs, no streetlights. If I didn't—no, I don't, I don't know this city."

"You're tired. We should have stopped somewhere along the way."

"There. See it—the looming shadow—the Telefónica Building, thirteen storeys. During the day as white as the Tower of Babel."

Alexandre pulls up across from the ghosting Telefónica. "This is El Hotel Gran Vía. I'll get us rooms and hire a guard for the station wagon. Stay inside. Lock the doors. Hands on your Bolos."

"Our introduction to Madrid has certainly been biblical," Sheila suggests.

"What part of the Bible?" Pat wants to keep them talking, hear their voices in the dark.

"I don't know. Is Masada mentioned in the Bible?" Sheila answers a question with a question.

"Do you mean King Herod's fortress?" Dorothy plays the question game.

"Yes, that's the one."

"But it was built on a mountain. Wasn't it, Shale?" Dorothy has recruited the last player.

"Still is." Shale keeps her eyes on the street. "What's left of it.

On a plateau at the edge of the Judean Desert, overlooking the Dead Sea."

"Masada, Madrid—the only thing they have in common is Ma." Dorothy laughs.

"Not so," Shale says gravely. "Madrid sits on a plateau of sand and clay overlooking the River Manzanares. Masada was under siege by the Romans. Madrid is under siege by forces that include Italians."

"What happened to Masada?" Pat asks in a small voice.

"The Romans destroyed it," Dorothy says softly while looking at Shale for confirmation, which comes in the form of a nod.

"They can't destroy what they can't find. That's why we're here." Pat slaps the back of the driver's seat.

"And they can't hide the truth. We're here to tell the world." Sheila gives Pat a hug, mindful of the Bolo resting in her lap.

It is just before dawn, and with the increase of light comes the realization that there are people walking the streets. Some dressed in heavy coats and hats. Some in evening clothes.

"Look—up ahead." Pat is the first to notice what Shale has been watching for some time. "Who are those people? Are they workers?"

"Gatos," Shale says.

"Cats? Where?"

"Madrileños call themselves 'cats.' Have for centuries." Shale is glad for the opportunity to change the subject. "Some believe it symbolizes their natural grace and agility. Others think it's because they like the nightlife, like to roam around after dark."

"I know the word 'gatos.' But what is Madrileños?" Pat asks.

"Simply, a native of Madrid. Like a Londoner or a Parisian."

Startled by banging on the window, they are relieved to see Alexandre at the driver's door.

"Our Madrileño," says Pat. "Or a tomcat." She giggles. "Just joking."

"All set. Grab your luggage." Alexandre's words have them on the sidewalk in minutes, where he hands out room keys. "Go into the lobby. There are bellhops by the stairs. The elevators don't work." He gets in behind the wheel.

"Where are you going?"

"There's a secure compound behind the hotel for the

station wagon.

"Do you want us to cover the car windows?" Pat is climbing into the back to pull the curtains hung from clothesline wire.

"Yes, do. No need to advertise what we're carrying, not even to the guards. The black market is thriving here." Alexandre starts the station wagon. "We'll meet at noon in the dining room and make plans." He drives up the street and turns, disappearing around the curved corner of the grand hotel.

☙☙☙☙

By the time the compatriots meet for lunch, Alexandre has set up meetings with the University of Madrid's Chief Librarian and Archivist, and the University Chancellor. He has also telephoned Dr. Abbot's contact at the Committee for Artistic Treasures, Director Timoteo Pérez Rubio, to introduce himself and Shale while offering Pat's services. He arranged for them to meet the Director the following afternoon.

Dorothy and Sheila arrive in the dining room obviously excited. Before Alexandre can reveal his well-laid plans, Dorothy announces that they have met with The Canadian Press reporter Fred Griffin in the hotel café. In the next few days, before he goes home for Christmas, Fred is taking them on a walking tour of Madrid. And not as tourists, Sheila adds.

"Is this man leading you into danger?" is Alexandre's response.

Dorothy sees only concern on Alexandre's face. "He knows the ropes and he's going to introduce Sheila around."

Reassured, Alexandre lays out their schedule for the morrow, after which he makes an offer, "So, today, I will be your tour guide. We will explore my Madrid and see what is left of it, including my apartment."

"You must experience the hotel café in the basement." Sheila seems bemused. "It is a special kind of bedlam. The foreign journalists have taken it over. They talk and write and talk waiting for a line to be available across the street in the Telefónica Building so they can dispatch their stories. And then there are the novelists secreted at their favourite corner tables."

"Sounds like a place for refreshment when we return." Alexandre surveys their attire, especially their shoes before standing to lead the way.

"While we're out and about, we should try and find Hazen and his doctor," Pat suggests.

"By all means, we'll stop at the front desk and see what the concierge knows."

Starting out along Gran Vía, they are amazed to see people lined up for the post office and the cinema, despite the percussion of artillery shells overhead. They walk the streets skirting the craters and the barricades. As they enter what would normally be a leafy neighbourhood of grand homes, they find yet another lineup outside of 36 Principe de Vergara. Alexandre taps the last man in the line on the shoulder and asks where the queue leads.

"This is it," he tells the women. "Can you believe it?"

"Only if we knew what 'it' was."

"The Servicio Canadiense de Transfusion de Sangre— the headquarters for Hazen and his doctor. These people are waiting to give blood."

"Then we'll wait with them." Shale steps up behind the last man.

Once they have made their contribution, they are free to search for Hazen throughout the enormous ground floor apartment. Disappointment is their lot. Hazen is delivering blood to some of Madrid's fifty-six hospitals.

"My apartment is not far from here if you're not too light-headed to walk." Alexandre will be glad to leave behind the needles and blood-filled borosilicate glass tubes.

As they move farther away from the tree-lined boulevard, there is increasingly more destruction. The sight is appalling and the constant mortar fire is nerve-wracking—all meant to break the spirit of the Madrileños. And yet there are lines of washing strung between the few standing walls: everyday flags waving at the housewives who search among the ruins for the objects that once defined their lives.

They cross into yet another district of wide boulevards. Alexandre points to a five-storey brick building. The windows are blown out, the roof is caved in over one corner, and the lobby doors are missing—remarkably untouched compared to its neighbours, attested to by the steady stream of people coming and going.

"I did lock the door to my apartment when I left. Do you think it did any good?" Irony is all Alexandre can manage at the moment.

"Good, yes, most probably. I can only assume these people in your building are homeless." Dorothy reframes his question.

The lobby is free of trash and swept clean. Alexandre looks around. "An improvement, I'd say." Bedding is neatly folded and stacked in a corner. As they climb to the third floor, it is clear the staircase has been tended to as well.

The door to 312 is closed. Alexandre tries the handle. The door opens on two women and four children with frightened eyes. He addresses them kindly, explaining that this is his apartment, that he doesn't intend to stay, but he would like to look for some of his possessions.

Alexandre goes directly to the room that holds his library. There, he finds a boy and girl, adolescents, reading. Reading his translated copies of Stevenson's *Dr. Jekyll and Mr. Hyde*, and George Sand's *Indiana*. The room is as he left it, except for the young people sprawled on the floor.

"Do you like them, the books?" he asks.

"Better than school," the girl says. The boy nods.

"Who are you?" the boy asks.

"The owner of this apartment."

"Oh, are you kicking us out?"

"If I did, where would you go?"

"Puerto Del Sol. We'd sleep in the tram station with all the others."

"Too many others. Some bad," the girl adds.

"Well, there's still a great many books to read, so you better stay here."

"Tell me something?" the girl asks.

"Yes, what is it?"

"Why does this man, George Sand, write a woman's story?"

"Because he is a she. The writer's real name is Aurore Dupin."

"This is something they do in France?"

"And other countries, yes. Not so much anymore. Not since the war."

The girl gives thoughtful attention to the cover of the novel.

"Will you watch over my books?" Alexandre wants them to have something to care about, something that matters in the chaos of their lives. And what better something than books.

"Yes," they say in unison.

Alexandre goes to a shelf and retrieves two books: Santiago Ramón y Cajal's *Manual de Anatomia Patológica General*, and Dr. Bacteria's *Vacation Stories*, science fiction stories written by the Noble Prize winner Ramón y Cajal.

Alexandre joins the others in the hall.

"What are you looking for?" Shale asks him.

"Nothing, other than these books. Long before I left Madrid, I sent anything of value to my agent in London. And Felipe is keeping some things for me, as well." He opens the door to a room at the end of the hall. "I just wanted to see."

They leave the new tenants to their new lives.

"Where to now?" Dorothy inquires.

"I've seen enough." Alexandre is resigned to the realization that Madrid is no longer his city. "Bedlam can't be any worse."

ꙮꙮ

Alexandre halts the SHE Gang at the door to the hotel café. "Please don't use my name here. Call me Santiago Ramón; it's the name I've registered under with the front desk. My brother expects me to be in Madrid. I want to disappoint him."

They enter and are greeted by Fred Griffin. "Hello, Dorothy, hello, Sheila. These are your friends?"

"Yes." Dorothy steps into the role of hostess. "Fred Griffin, I would like you to meet Dr. Grace Clifden, Dr. Santiago Ramón, and"— Dorothy loops her arm through Pat's arm — "PK Page, Pat for short."

"Glad to meet you." Fred turns to Dorothy. "You keep auspicious company, friends with letters before their names.

"Let's sit over there." Dorothy points to a table away from the raucous voices gathered around an American with an even bigger voice.

Sheila had disappeared during the introductions, only to return bearing a tray of drinks. She hands them around while Fred gathers up his papers from another table.

Shale is interested in the mess he has laid on their table. "What have you got there, Fred? They look like leaflets."

"Indeed they are—signed by Franco himself, spewing his usual lies claiming that the Jews have taken over Spain's banks and Soviet Russia commands the Republicans."

"Where did you get them?"

"They fell from the sky. My landlady says the devil is tearing up his diary. In this case, her devil flies a Junkers 52."

Pat has been surreptitiously watching the boisterous table. "I always thought writers were quiet, bookish types. Who are your cohorts?"

"Well, the Brit is George Orwell, the Frenchy is André Malraux, and then there's the ubiquitous Yanks, Herb Matthews for *The New York Times,* John Dos Passos, and Ernest Hemingway."

☙☙☙☙

Alexandre, Shale, and Dorothy retrace their steps down Gran Vía, passing into the district of luxury homes.

Dorothy seems preoccupied, so much so that Alexandre has to take her arm as they negotiate several barricades. It takes a shell burst nearby to wake her up. The bang above their heads materializes as a white cloud. High and far enough away, the shock wave doesn't throw them to the ground.

"Dorothy, what's on your mind?" Alexandre asks now that he has her attention.

She studies him, realizing that he is no longer The Brother to her. "Sheila. Griffin has taken her to meet Emil Kléber, leader of the International Column in Madrid. Fred wants Sheila to focus her dispatches on the International Brigades' efforts. He's talking about a trip to Albacete, where the Internationals are headquartered."

"What? Albacete? How?"

"That's not the half of it. He's suggested she train with the Women's Militia. Then do an in-depth magazine piece."

"And what does Sheila think of his proposals?"

"Oh, Sheila—she may be barely five feet tall, but her spirit is bold. Once they've met with the charismatic Kléber, Sheila's going to try and find a mono, the militia uniform. The way she described it to me, it sounds like a mechanic's overall."

"And you're worried." Alexandre stops before an ornate wrought-iron gate.

"Not worried, so much, as working an angle."

Shale has been quietly listening to this exchange. "Come on, spill the beans." Despite her casual language, Shale has picked up on an undercurrent in Dorothy's telling. She suspects Dorothy is holding out on Alexandre, precisely because he is Dr. Castro.

"All right, I want to go to Albacete and look for Jean Watts."

"Why?" Alexandre is being Dr. Castro in his use of the single-word questioning method of interrogation.

"To celebrate her birthday. She'll be twenty-seven soon."

Shale and Alexandre share a look that says there is more to this, but now is not the time.

Alexandre pushes open the gate. The Chancellor awaits them, and Alexandre wants their work in Madrid completed as soon as possible. He fears the ladies have come under some kind of spell. This is no place for them. Visions of Felicia Browne fill his head, so much so that he has to give it a shake when the maid opens the front door.

They are ushered into a sumptuous sitting room all brocade and picture hangers. Taken aback by the naked walls, the group remains standing in the middle of the room. Finally, Alexandre speaks. "It would appear the Committee for Artistic Treasures has come to the rescue."

"Yes, indeed, Dr. Castro." The Chancellor stands in the arched doorway.

"Chancellor." Alexandre holds out his hand. "A great pleasure to see you."

"And you. My walls seem forlorn in the presence of your friends."

"Let me introduce them," Alexandre offers.

"Yes, of course. Give me a moment; there is another member of our enclave."

The Chancellor returns with the university's head librarian. Alexandre is pleased to see the most knowledgeable of all his colleagues, especially when it comes to the university precinct. An architect before accepting a position as Chief Librarian meant to build the library's collection, "The Head" is a special friend.

Even before introductions, Alexandre must ask, "Are you well? And your family?"

Once they are settled around a low table filled with gilt decorated Limoges china and a cake stand of pastries, Alexandre presents their mission.

All The Head can say is "You came back, Alexandre. You came back and brought your own brigade."

Alexandre examines his coffee, and then looks up. "My friends are a force to be reckoned with."

The Head retrieves his briefcase and reveals a folded blueprint. He lays it out on a side table. "Some time ago, I created an architectural plan of the university campus from the many disparate documents whole and fragmented that have rested in the library undisturbed for decades."

"Brilliant." Alexandre claps him on the back, as only a friend can in front of The Chancellor.

The Head smiles, acknowledging Alexandre's enthusiasm. "These snaking lines are tunnels that run under the buildings, connecting them all." He invites his audience of four to examine the plan more closely.

"We've moved hundreds of boxes of books and documents to the tunnels. That said, the campus buildings are shell-shocked, hollow men barely standing. And, of course, the fighting has escalated. Saints be praised, we still have access to the tunnels through the Philosophy Building. And here's the best part: the tunnel that runs under the Library Building has a shaft that surfaces in front of the Archives Vault in the library's basement."

The Head pauses to give them time to form their own ideas,

and then turns to Alexandre, "I am relieved that you have helping hands. My assistants are doing everything they can do, moving the boxes of books and papers between tunnels according to where the shells are falling above. And to make matters worse, those barbaric Fascists have brought in German tanks."

The Head leaves them to ponder the blueprint while he pours himself another coffee.

"How do we access the Philosophy Building?" Alexandre finally asks, even more reluctant now to involve the women in the mission.

Shale joins The Head at the low table, her gilt rimmed cup extended. Before he can answer Alexandre's query, Shale, fearing the worst, asks if he knows the whereabouts of the university's archaeological artifacts.

"Would you rescue these as well, Dr. Clifden?"

"As many as I can."

"I see. Perhaps we should all confer over another cup of excellent coffee." He waits for them to settle. "There are a small number of artifacts in the Archives Vault, moved there at the beginning of the battle and siege in November. I believe these artifacts are the most important of the collection, primarily prehistoric."

"When? How?" Alexandre's look is riveting, perhaps a little too penetrating for his friend, who has just raised a polvorón to his mouth.

The Head puts the rich cookie back on his plate. "With permission from General Kléber. If he agrees, he will assign a protection detail."

There is that name again: Kléber. "And you can arrange this, Mateo?"

"Yes, Alexandre. Now eat your cake."

ᏯᏯᏯ

Pat enters the hotel café, stops, and surveys the room. Journalists occupy all but two tables, and the boisterous group has returned to claim the centre of the room.

She straightens her shoulders, feeling her silk blouse sigh across her shoulder blades. Dressed to meet the Director of the

Committee for Protection of Artistic Treasures, she has chosen from her Paris purchases the magenta blouse, grey skirt with side-pleats, and black cape jacket.

Crossing the room to a vacant table under the sidewalk level windows, Pat does not go unnoticed. She has barely removed her jacket when one of the loud men approaches her table.

"Hi, I'm John. Please join us."

Pat demurs, aware she is seriously outnumbered. "Thank you. That's very kind, but I'm waiting for friends."

"Wait with us. We don't bite. Well, hardly ever."

She laughs. "A pack of wolves, I suspect."

It is his turn to laugh. He takes the opportunity to sit down across from her.

"Yes, writers can be wolfish on occasion. Not easy to feed oneself in this profession," he says.

"Profession—are you a scribe or a scribbler?"

John howls like a wolf at a full moon. Finally, he says, "Impertinent young thing, aren't you? Come to a party at the Hotel Florida tonight. You'll fit right in."

"You didn't answer my question." Pat recognizes a diversion when she hears it.

"Both. You'll have to come tonight to find out more." He pats her hand and takes his leave.

Happily, Fred and Sheila arrive, full of news. They make a beeline for Pat's table. John does not hide his interest in the new development.

No greeting from Fred. The first thing he says is "Sheila was a hit with Kléber. When she suggested she train with the Women's Militia, he looked ready to give her a Russian bear hug."

Pat is obviously distracted.

Fred glances at the loud table. "What's up, Pat?"

"I just got invited to a party at the Hotel Florida by a man called, John."

Fred scrutinizes the table of foreign correspondents. "Believe me, you do not want to go there. They'll eat you alive. And that's just the prostitutes."

Pat's look of shock is mirrored by Sheila.

"Besides the fact that the Florida is only a dozen blocks from the street fighting, that crew depends too much on booze and bravado," he says.

There is silence until Dorothy arrives at the table. "We're back. Pat, you look lovely. Shale and Alexandre are waiting for you in the lobby."

Dorothy takes Pat's place. She notices the interest from the centre table. "Why don't we have some lunch in the dining room. I want to hear all about your meeting this morning."

Heading east on Gran Vía, Alexandre has a lady on each arm. All three, dressed in their Parisian finery, are turning heads as they march in step. The look of determination on their faces discourages gawking.

Their destination is the Basílica de San Francisco el Grande where the art committee is collecting, documenting and storing works of art from churches, convents, and private homes. Pat is destined to be one of many volunteers cataloguing thousands of pieces of art in duplicate and triplicate.

In November, the Fascists had bombed the Museo del Prado and the Liria Palace. The Prado staff had moved all the museum's art to the basement and sandbagged the main floor. The building was damaged, but the art was not. The rescued works are now being prepared by restorers for transport by truck to Valencia. During the air raid, the United Youth of the Spanish Communist Party had saved the Dukes of Alba's famous art collection in the Liria Palace from destruction. Nevertheless, making safe Spain's cultural artifacts is still a race against time. Pat's help will be welcomed.

On entering the Plaza de San Francisco, they pause at the sight of the Basílica rising out of the Square, tier on tier to a majestic dome.

"Largest dome in Spain," Alexandre murmurs. "Larger than Saint Paul's in London."

"We humans have been fascinated by rock since the first time we picked up a stone and hurled it at a predator." Shale has always been aware of the mystique of stone structures.

"And this is where the Committee is storing the art? Hell of a target for a bomber." Pat is calculating her chances of survival. "You know, they dropped nine incendiary bombs on the Prado."

"Franco has yet to target a church. Not that he respects religion—he respects his reputation more." Alexandre senses Pat's reluctance.

"Reassuring," Pat notes without conviction as she moves toward the dark wood of the carved doors.

They are ushered into a busy room, busy but quiet, one type-writer surrounded by long wooden tables laden with documents under the control of silent, studious clerks. Pat has taken a step back behind Alexandre and Shale. Suddenly, she feels shy. It has occurred to her that she will be on her own here, among people who speak a different language.

The onlookers are greeted by a bespectacled man wearing a broad smile. "Dr. Castro?" He extends a hand.

"Yes, indeed. And my colleagues, Dr. Clifden and Miss Page."

"Welcome, welcome. So kind of you to take an interest in our cause."

"Not at all. Yourself and the Committee are saviours."

"Knights in shining armour," Pat ventures.

The Director appears nonplussed, and then smiles at Pat. "Welcome to the legion. No round tables, I'm afraid."

They all laugh. The clerks raise their eyes to the sound, pleased to see their beleaguered 'líder' animated.

"Director Pérez Rubio, may I ask the state of the Archaeological Museum?"

The Director's face turns scarlet with anger. "The Fascists bombed the Archaeological and Anthropological Museums, the National Library, and the Fine Arts Academy. Since the first aerial attacks in November, we have moved the most important objects and improved protection of the buildings."

Shale listens intently to The Director, and Alexandre is reminded of why she came to Spain in the first place, despite the danger. Kindred spirits, he thinks.

Shale shakes her head. "They can't destroy our ancestral memory. It's in each and every one of us, no matter."

"Señor." The typist is standing behind The Director. "I must leave. I'm sorry, but I'm unwell."

"Yes, of course. Victor will accompany you."

"Thank you."

The Director turns to Pat. "Do you type, Miss Page?"

"Yes. Given my language skills, transcription is a good fit for me." Pat is pleased there is something she can do to help.

☾☾☾

Alexandre and Shale meet The Head in the Gran Vía Hotel Bar for a quick drink before he takes them to a rendezvous with Emil Kléber.

"The General seems bemused by the task you have set yourselves," The Head remarks as he looks along the bar at them. "His headquarters may be in the university's Philosophy and Letters Building, but he is unequivocal . . . his destiny awaits."

With this pronouncement, they leave the bar for the busy Gran Vía thoroughfare.

"Kléber? Emil Kléber?" Shale tries the name on. "Who is he really?"

"A mystery" is The Head's answer. "Slavic look about him. There are rumours—he fought with the Canadian Expeditionary Force in Siberia, fought with the Communists in China. A charismatic enigma, but a damn good General. Madrid's good fortune."

"Where are you taking us, Mateo?" Alexandre had expected to find The General in a café or bar somewhere off Gran Vía.

"The Chancellor has offered to host our meeting. Ostensibly, his home has become his university office."

"I see, pleasant turn of events. And the coffee is superb."

They walk briskly, fully aware of the battle at Segovia Bridge. A reminder that General Kléber is tasked with defending not only University City, but the whole of Madrid. North of Madrid his front line extends into the Sierra de Guadarrama, where Republicans of many nationalities are repelling the Nationalist forces, especially along the vital Escorial Road.

Upon arrival, the maid leads them through the house to the garden terrace. Apparently, The General is listening to the sound of guns, shells, and bombs, while The Chancellor sips his coffee. She opens her hand, revealing two white balls of cotton—she does not want to hear the war.

For a moment, they stand at the French doors, studying the scene.

"I suspect The General is monitoring his territory," Alexandre concludes.

"Reconnaissance," is The Head's word for it, spoken as he opens the doors.

"Buenas tardes," Alexandre addresses The Chancellor, who rises to meet them.

Introductions conclude, and as if on cue, the maid appears with a tray of cups, a carafe of coffee, and plates of pastries. As the maid serves them, Shale takes the opportunity to size-up The General. Strong features, dark hair touched with silver, robust build—what you might expect, except for the intelligent eyes and the perfect American English. A tilt of the head suggests The General is ready to do business.

The General waves the maid away. "What is so important that you would risk entering a war zone?"

Alexandre puts his coffee aside. "Your war zone was a university before power-hungry Franco decided to devour his own. A place of research where cutting-edge discoveries are chipping away at the human burden, or at least they were. This work is documented and stored in the Archives Vault. This knowledge is meant for world good."

"Mortars have no respect for knowledge, good or bad. This is the world, as we know it. And it is a dangerous place."

"Well, General, you risk your life to save Spain and the world. I will do the same."

"And what of Dr. Clifden?" He turns his magnetic gaze on Shale.

"There are artifacts stored in the vault that symbolize the human mind through time—every human mind through tens of thousands of years. These objects, fashioned by human hands, set us apart, define the kind of being we are. We cannot afford to lose them."

General Kléber starts to laugh, then roar. "Paper and stone—a child's game."

"A two thousand-year old Han Dynasty game meant to settle disputes. Do we have a dispute to settle?" Shale asks the General.

He laughs harder. "Dr. Clifden, I have no doubt who my enemy is and no doubt as to my duty. I must do what I must do, and so shall you."

He stands, pulls his jacket into place, and extends his hand to The Chancellor.

Turning to The Head, he says, "Tomorrow, 4:00 a.m., Philosophy and Letters. I'll send an escort. Until then, Dr. Castro, Dr. Clifden, keep your heads down." The General raises his right fist in the air, the Republican salute.

All Shale can think of is Rock Paper Scissors. She hopes the irony doesn't show in her eyes.

"Dr. Castro," The Chancellor lays claim to his duties, "what will you remove from the Archival Vault?"

"Primarily scientific research, especially from my own department. You see, Chancellor, before Dr. Peralta, Dr. Silva and I left Madrid on November tenth, we burned our research notes and papers."

"That seems rash." The Chancellor is unpleasantly surprised.

"The vault will also contain a letter from the State Intelligence Service—a ministerial order to the Dean of the Psychology Department to supply personnel capable of devising methods of enhanced interrogation. In other words, psychological torture." Alexandre is looking for signs that The Chancellor knew about this letter. Nothing is revealed.

"I see. You did not view this as an idle request. Ostensibly, it sent you and your colleagues into hiding. And you are concerned there are copies of your work in the vault."

"Certainly, it's dangerous knowledge in the wrong hands. Beyond that, the vault contains scientific breakthroughs that could be lost or destroyed. That would be a crime against humanity."

"And what will you do, once you have the documents? How can you keep them safe?" The Chancellor wants the whole picture. On one level he abhors the idea that this body of knowledge from his university will leave the country.

"The Smithsonian in Washington will give them sanctuary." Alexandre pauses, ready for remonstration.

The Chancellor's attention moves to Shale. "Dr. Clifden, you have confirmation?"

"Dr. Abbot was consulted and agreed before we left London. He recognizes, as do we, the importance of this undertaking."

The Chancellor blinks rapidly, momentarily startled by Shale's straightforward answer.

The Head catches Alexandre's eye and lowers his gaze slightly, acknowledging the acumen of Alexandre's new friend.

"The Smithsonian's protection extends to the archaeological artifacts?" The Chancellor is succinct.

"Yes, of course; however, I intend to consult with Timoteo Pérez Rubio and the Committee for The Requisition and Protection of Artistic Treasures."

Alexandre decides to lighten the discussion, "One of our group is working for The Committee, as a volunteer."

The Chancellor looks from one to the other. "You two make a good team. I am reassured. But now you must excuse me, I have a meeting with Josep Renau, Director General of Fine Arts."

Well-played, Alexandre thinks, but lets it pass. "Ah, yes, Director Pérez Rubio's boss."

Shale checks the time by glancing at The Head's wristwatch. "We should be on our way," she explains that Director Pérez Rubio requires the members of his staff be accompanied through the streets of Madrid upon leaving the Basílica.

ꙮꙮꙮ

The hotel bar is quiet for a change. They find a table big enough for the five of them, their drinks, and their stories of the day. The telling is tinged with excitement rather than anxiety or fear. Alexandre does not trust the mood—is it a precursor to recklessness? With this thought uppermost in his mind, Sheila announces that she and Dorothy are leaving for Albacete in the morning. General Kléber has found room for them on a troop truck evacuating wounded and returning with more international volunteers. Apparently they will be expected to tend the wounded. The General doesn't miss an opportunity.

There is silence—not what Sheila expected. "I'll train with the recruits, while Dorothy interviews the brigaders."

"Well, say something," Dorothy demands.

"Don't go," Pat says. "We shouldn't be apart . . . we're a gang."

Sheila puts her arm around Pat's shoulder. "We all have jobs to do here in Spain. Anyway, General Kléber has made sure we're well protected."

"Perhaps," Dorothy says. "But he was best pleased that we have our own side arms." She refrains from saying so to the group, but suspects that her and Sheila will be taking care of themselves for the most part.

"Well, it would seem The General has become our patron saint. He's making it possible for us to start on the Archives Vault tomorrow." Alexandre keeps anticipation out of his voice.

"I don't know about saint, not the way he looks at Sheila." Dorothy places her hand over Sheila's, where it rests on the table. "I'm pretty sure he doesn't want to lose you until he knows where he stands—or more precisely lies, you know, lay of the land." Dorothy squeezes Sheila's hand.

Shale looks at the two of them, heads together. "Just make sure The General knows he'll have me to reckon with if something happens. If you don't tell him tomorrow, I will."

"By the way, I'm expropriating your suitcases," Alexandre says.

"What! So, we can't go? No matter, I'm taking my rucksack anyway." Dorothy sees The Brother of their kidnapper.

"No, of course not. We'll use them to transport the documents from the vault." Alexandre wonders about the look on Dorothy's face: What exists behind the eyes?

"What time do you leave? Can you walk Pat to work? We're expected to be at the university by 4:00 a.m." Shale suddenly realizes they are all abandoning Pat.

"Oh dear. The truck is scheduled to pick us up from here at midnight. Travelling by dark of night."

"I can go on my own. I know the way." Pat will not be treated like a child.

"I'm sure Fred would be happy to walk with you," Sheila offers. "I'll find him and invite him for a drink. What do you say?" Sheila is gone before they can respond.

Sheila and Fred appear, and minutes later, a waiter as well. Alexandre orders drinks all around to welcome Fred.

"Miss Page, may I accompany you to San Francisco El Grande, on the morrow?" Fred tips his hat.

"Well, Mr. Griffin, it appears you share more than a name with Mr. Astaire." Pat raises an eyebrow.

A successful tableau: the two of them smile at the uproar they have created at the table.

"It's kismet. You two are headed for the silver screen," Sheila prophesies.

"And here, I thought it was the Basílica that awaits." Fred sits in the chair provided by the waiter. "In the face of your news, it's good to laugh."

They watch and wait.

"The wounded being evacuated will be from the battle at University City two days ago, about the time you arrived." He sees the blank looks on their faces. "The Fascists decided to break the stalemate— an all-out attack with tanks and machine guns, German made and German manned. General Kléber's soldiers clobbered them. Heavy Fascist losses. Then the next day, Franco extended the attack to the northwest, mowing down villages in an attempt to take the Escorial Road." Fred reaches for his drink.

"Stalemate?" Shale asks.

"As you know, University City has been Madrid's battleground since November seventh." Fred looks around the table for signs of comprehension. He decides more is required. "The fighting has been ongoing and brutal. The Fascists took the Clinical Hospital, a huge, unfinished building, but in use, nevertheless, as a medical school and clinic. Now it's their headquarters. The government sent the Durruti Column of Anarchists from Barcelona to take back the Clinical Hospital and rout the Fascists. And they just about succeeded. On November nineteenth, the day the Anarchist leader, Buenaventura Durruti took a bullet, was the day the Republicans lost the Clinical Hospital yet again."

"The Republican government mobilized anarchists?" Pat is bewildered.

"Ask Miss Livesay about the roots of anarchism in workers'

parties." Fred looks to Dorothy. "I'm sure she's familiar with Spain's Anarcho Syndicalists—after all, she's a founding member of the Canadian League Against War and Fascism."

When Dorothy is not forthcoming, Fred picks up where he left off, "To make a long story short, the International Brigades are still at it. And it's become more like guerrilla warfare on both sides, than a field of battle."

"Yes?" Alexandre prods.

Fred puts his drink down. "It makes the campus even more dangerous for you. The battle lines are blurred. It's about ambush, hit-and-run, sniping. You need eyes in the back of your head. Preferably a set of eyes armed to the teeth." He laughs uproariously to dispel the sense of dread.

♋♋♋

Winter winds gust off the Sierra de Guadarrama as Dorothy and Sheila are helped into the back of the troop truck. The only protection from the penetrating cold is a thin canvas tarp and huddled bodies. The two women had said their goodbyes with hugs and tears. Holding Shale close, Dorothy had whispered in her ear, "I'll take care of Sheila." And Sheila had vowed that they had sent Shale's message to General Kléber with Fred as their messenger.

It is not a quiet departure: the rough ride of the truck on its solid rubber tires gives rise to cries and groans from under the tarp. Unsettled, Alex, Shale, and Pat take refuge in the hotel lobby. There is no comfort in the plush chairs, and even less in the silence. Companionship is restored by the concierge, who offers to have coffee brought to them. He has witnessed the midnight departure.

Four hours later, Alexandre and Shale are waiting in the lobby yet again, this time dressed head to toe in black. Their Mausers are hard against their ribs in shoulder holsters, courtesy of General Kléber. Neither of them has slept, but they're too nervy to notice.

The Head arrives in the lobby, having left the escort at the end of the block trying to stay warm by stamping their feet. Their billows of frosty breath combined with their stomping makes him think of a restless herd.

Alexandre and Shale meet him at the door. Mateo describes their route, impresses on them the need to move quickly and quietly, and more importantly, to stay in the middle of the escort.

They join the escort and leave immediately, the soldiers glad to be on the move. The band travel by moonlight, the city no longer civilized by electricity.

At the edge of the campus, the band must negotiate a prearranged path through the Republican trenches. Passwords are required. General Kléber chose the hour well—there is blessed silence. It makes the soldiers nervous. Silence is not to be trusted.

As they reach the Philosophy and Letters Building, bullets tear into the door in front of them. One of the soldiers orders them to take cover behind an abandoned truck. There is return fire from the closest Republican trench. The soldier quickly confers with The Head, who in a crouch leads them along the wall away from the door. The band pass behind a toppled statue of Cervantes and duck down a set of stairs. When they reach the bottom, The Head unlocks a door. He takes a lantern from a hook on the wall, lights it, and starts down the staircase to the basement. A soldier also lights a lantern and the escort heads upstairs to report in.

In the furthest wall of the basement is another door. Mateo unlocks it, invites them to enter, and relocks it. "This tunnel leads to the library. It's remarkably spacious, so Xandre you won't have to crouch. Not all the tunnels would give you head room. Luckily, none of my staff are tall. Having to crouch while carrying boxes of books would only add more hardship to what are already bleak days spent like moles waiting for their burrows to collapse."

"Small blessing," Alexandre remarks.

Mateo gives him a grin, turns and leads the way. They are assailed by echoes only: the big guns silent before dawn.

Ahead, after what Shale calculates as about ten city blocks, the shaft is made apparent by a metal ladder attached to the tunnel wall. As they reach it, the trapdoor above is revealed. Mateo hands Alexandre the lantern and swings up the ladder, then lifts the door and slides it back. Remarkably, it barely makes a sound. Mateo has smoothed the way for them. He takes back the lantern.

Alexandre and Shale ascend from darkness into light. Mateo is standing in a large room containing a vault door flanked by shelves. The vault itself is built into the foundation. It would appear they have reached the tunnel by a sub-basement and have now accessed the actual library basement. There are reading tables graced with green-shade reading lights and tall oil lamps. Shale feels very much at home for the first time since arriving in Madrid.

Mateo labours over the vault's dial lock, turns a large metal wheel, then pushes a long handle to the side. Grabbing the wheel with both hands, he pulls the door open. At this point, all he is willing to say is artifacts and significant documents are stored in the vault according to Faculties; everything else is on the shelves in the room.

He disappears inside and returns with a large tin file box, sets it on a reading table, removes the glass chimney from a nearby oil lamp, and lights the wick. "Psychology Department 1936. Get started, and I'll bring out 1935 to work on, and the Archaeology Department 1936 for Shale." Mateo starts back to the vault.

"I'll light more lamps," Shale offers.

Alexandre brings a lamp to his place in front of the box and releases the snaps on the tin lid.

Shale and Mateo create circles of light for themselves and their boxes.

These moments of academic peace are bliss for the three of them. Too soon, they are reminded of the hell that awaits, as mortar shells explode their silence. They focus on the work at hand, rather than think about what would happen if the library took a direct hit. Mateo reassures them that both sides are intent on taking down their rivals' headquarters in the Philosophy and Letters Building and the Clinical Hospital. The unassuming Library Building is momentarily of no interest.

Finally, Mateo stretches and breaks the quietude. "Did you find the letter, Alexandre? The one from the State Intelligence Service?"

"Yes, and a handwritten list of possible candidates."

'Oh, that's disappointing—the list, I mean. It signals compliance. Am I right in assuming that you, Felipe and Reinaldo are on the list?"

"Yes."

"How are Felipe and Reinaldo? Have you heard from them?" Mateo redirects the moment.

"Felipe is in France. Naldo is in Switzerland. With their families."

"Glad to hear it."

Shale is aware there is something unsaid between the men. Perhaps it's a matter of 'what you don't know won't hurt you.' Knowledge, she thinks, looking around her—a double-edged sword.

With the passing hours, the air in the room becomes fetid. Mateo checks his watch and decides they should seek fresh air. "How are you getting along?"

"Very well." Alexandre doesn't look up.

"Given the fact that this is a windowless room and we're lighting it with oil lamps, we should take a break."

"Where?" Shale asks.

"Upstairs. I must meet with my staff. They will have made coffee. Don't expect Italian Moka Express. Stewed coffee in enamel pots on camp stoves is our brew."

"Anything resembling coffee would be appreciated." Shale turns down the wick in her lamp, extinguishing the flame.

"We could stretch our legs by carrying some boxes of books for you, Mateo." Alexandre looks to Shale for agreement.

"Done. The sooner I have the day's work in progress, the sooner I can return to our task here." Mateo leads the way holding the lantern high.

After coffee and their turn as beasts of burden, Alexandre and Shale go back to the vault room and leave Mateo to his duties as The Head.

When they finish reviewing a box, they lay the documents they have selected on top of the files, replace the lid, return the box to the vault, and extract another tin box. Shale periodically consults Alexandre when she has doubts about her translation of the Spanish text to English. This becomes the rhythm of their afternoon, and afternoons to come, except when they break the tedium by trading life stories. Shale has come to realize that Alexandre is fascinated by her childhood spent in the Smithsonian. She is convinced his interest is more professional than personal. While she is interested in his pursuit of academics, especially given the mindset and temperament of his brother, El Comandante. She also wonders why he has not married.

᧥᧥᧥

At the end of the day, Fred Griffin presents himself at the Basílica, ostensibly to collect Pat but, being the journalist he is, to also chat up The Director and collect information. He would like to know what will become of all the artworks once they are documented. To that end, Pérez Rubio is tight-lipped. Fred hopes to have better luck elsewhere in his hunt for a story.

Once on the pavement, he asks Pat to accompany him to meet Dr. Bethune at what has become Servicio Canadiense de Transfusion de Sangre. "A mouthful," he quips. "Imagine that lettered on the side of an ambulance."

They arrive at 36 Principe de Vergara to find only a few donors lined up outside the door. Fred is encouraged: perhaps Dr. Bethune will be free to talk. Pat is going to look for Hazen Sise, with the intention of inviting him for a drink.

Sometime later, the three of them arrive at the Gran Vía Hotel to find Shale and Alexandre already ensconced in the bar. Hagen is a novel addition to what is becoming their regular table.

"Just the man." Alexandre puts out his hand.

"I try to be." Hazen shakes the proffered hand.

"I have an ambulance packed with medical supplies. Could you make use of it?" Alexandre asks.

"Of course." Hagen sits down hard. "I think I need a drink."

"Consider it a Christmas present. The ambulance, not the drink." Alexandre summons the waiter.

"I'm speechless, but I'm sure the Doctor won't be."

"The ambulance is parked in the hotel's compound." Alexandre reaches into his pocket for the keys. " You could take it tonight, if you like."

Fred has just witnessed his next story, to be dispatched from the still-standing Telefónica Building that evening.

☙☙☙☙

Leaving University City after a long day in the library vault, Alexandre and Shale skirt the Student Residence and enter Parque del Oeste. There are four Republican Columns and Brigades patrolling the Park. The Passes issued by General Kléber to "The Savants," his pet name for Alexandre and Shale, provide the pair with a small sense of security in the dark woods. Remaining among the trees while passing the infantry barracks, they reach the residential district of Moncloa-Aravaca.

As they negotiate the bombed-out streets, the pair is aware of figures among the ruined buildings. It is apparent they are being encircled. Alexandre motions to Shale and they make a dash for what's left of a small cobbler's shop. Back-to-back, they pull out their Mauser Bolos.

"Provocadores Fascistas," Alexandre whispers.

"Fifth Columnists, here?" Shake asks.

"Playing cat and mouse with the militias."

Shale can see shapes creeping closer. Someone shouts for them to come out, to surrender. Shale readies her pistol. Alexandre shakes his head.

There is gunfire. Alexandre shakes his head again. "A test. They don't know who we are, if we're armed."

There is a charge on Shale's side. She waits, and then fires a warning shot that has their assailants diving for cover.

When the Fascist sympathizers return fire, Alexandre joins in, aiming to cause damage. Being a good shot, he hits his mark more than once.

The ruins go silent. Not for long—the cats have found the mice. Armed citizens, one of Madrid's militias, surround the Fifth Columnists. It turns into a real firefight. Alexandre and Shale keep their heads down.

The militia doesn't take prisoners. They strip the dead Fascist provocateurs of their weapons and valuables. Then leave.

Alexandre and Shale go unacknowledged, left amid the ruins and the carnage.

⊆⊇⊆⊇⊆⊇

The streets of Madrid are never deserted. Fred, in his walks to and from the Basílica, finds different routes and different Madrids. He is grateful Pat is such a keen explorer and observer. Recently he discovered that she keeps a journal, filling it with poetry and sketches. She has been reluctant to give him access to her musings. But today, he sits in the Plaza de San Francisco, the Basílica towering above him, its grandeur lost as he carefully turns the pages in the sketchbook Pat had presented to him on the steps of Basílica de San Francisco el Grande before disappearing through the doors to her job.

The sketches are stark reminders of what this young woman has witnessed. She has forgotten nothing: women and children sitting outside a rough-hewn stone fortification that serves as barricade and bomb shelter in the neighbourhood of Argüelles; a crowd of men gazing skyward, watching a dogfight between Republican and Nationalist airplanes; boys carrying lunch pots, standing in the street studying a poster taller than themselves of a huge bomb being dropped on Madrid as a white dove flies away. EVACUAD MADRID is the slogan, telling them to run away, far away from their homes.

The poem, below a sketch of the sandbagged storefront of a FARMACIA & PERFUMERIA, does not fail to remark on the irony. Pat has titled the poem "Not Enough." The first lines amplify the imperative of the title:

Not Enough   Perfume in the world   To hide the smell
Of Burning Flesh

The quality of her language and the visceral depth of her observations amaze him; after all, she is only twenty years old.

⊆⊇⊆⊇⊆⊇

Today, the walls shake. The vault ceased to be a sanctuary when the tanks arrived at dawn. Alexandre and Shale have picked up the pace of their work and conversation: talking blocks some of the intrusive sound while giving them comfort.

Shale has retrieved another box, this time a wooden one from a shelf to the right of the vault. She is looking for the last pages of an essay she had found earlier in a tin box.

She sits for a moment and contemplates Alexandre. "It's obvious why I chose archaeology as an academic pursuit"— she waits for him to look up— "but less obvious why you chose psychology."

He finally raises his head. "Is that an observation or a question?"

"Both . . . one generates the other."

"I'm a lapsed neuroscientist."

Shale remains quiet, an expectant air about her.

"I was going to follow in the footsteps of Santiago Ramón y Cajal . . . pathologist, histologist, neuroanatomist. I enrolled in the Faculty of Physiology, but I didn't find the dead held my interest. So, I decided to study the living."

"My pals were always the dead. They spoke volumes . . . never hesitated to contradict me."

Alexandre smiles at Shale. "You are the most well-adjusted enigma I've ever met."

"Well, thank you, Dr. Castro, for the compliment from your esteemed self."

He laughs loud enough to drown out the guns.

"Being a man of your time and place, why have you not married?"

Alexandre stops smiling. "As audacious as any American I've met." He shakes his head. "I could ask you the same question."

"In my case, it's obvious," Shale replies.

"Not to me," Alexandre disagrees. "You are neither grotesque nor unbalanced."

"Is that your professional opinion?"

"Simply an observation."

"Well, what you've missed is the cultural component. I chose my profession over conventional servitude. Archaeology, as a profession, does not lend itself to domestic bliss."

"Would your male colleagues agree?"

"Some would, but most lead double lives, especially those in the field, the excavators. But, of course, they have a homemaker waiting for them, emphasis on 'home' and 'waiting.'" Shale studies him studying the file laid out before him on the table.

"Life unfolds" are his last words before The Head enters with an offer of coffee and a summons from General Kléber."

"Here, drink your coffee and then I'll take you through the tunnels to The General." Mateo joins them. "Are you making progress?"

"Yes, within the next few days, we'll bring suitcases that we can fill and take away." Alexandre sips his strong, boiled coffee.

"Not without an escort. You two, carrying suitcases, would be prime targets for looters among other villains." Mateo looks from Alexandre to Shale for concurrence.

"Well"—Shale rises—"we can put it to The General."

"Do you know what he wants?" Alexandre drains his cup and sets it on the table near Mateo.

"Not a clue. He confides in no one, least of all me."

Down the shaft and through the tunnels, they can't help but feel they're playing truant. Until they reach what was once the office of the Dean of Philosophy and Letters. Along the way, Alexandre is appalled at the damage to the marble floors and fine wood panelling of the halls and offices they pass.

General Kléber has made himself at home. As well as the Dean's impressive antique desk covered with maps, the room has two leather club chairs and a cot.

By way of welcome, The General leaves Alexandre and Shale to stand before the desk while he occupies the Dean's throne behind it. He gets right to the point, "You were compromised last night."

"We were set upon by Fifth Columnists, yes," Alexandre replies.

"You returned fire?"

"Yes," Shale confirms. "And we made it count."

"But a militia made the kill, and rescued you."

"Where are we going with this?" Shale had enough of cat and mouse last night.

"I can't afford a daily escort for you."

"We don't require one." Alexandre is firm.

"Perhaps you don't, Dr. Castro, but Dr. Clifden should not be here. Campus de Moncloa is no place for a woman."

Before Shale can disagree, Alexandre speaks, "Dr. Clifden has worked in a score of dangerous regions around the world. She is tried and true. Well prepared to be here."

A Cheshire cat look crosses General Kléber's handsome face.

Shale decides to set the parameters. "We're close to being finished, but we will require help removing the documents from the library and the campus. We'll have six bulging suitcases to transport to the Hotel de Gran Vía."

"How close?"

"A week." Shale looks to Alexandre for confirmation. "I'm preparing to wrap a collection of significant prehistoric artifacts dating from eighteen thousand years ago. Would you care to see them?"

"Perhaps. But significant history is being made as we speak. And my role is assured."

A ghost of a smile crosses Shale's face. "General Kléber, I appreciate your concern for my safety, but the world is a dangerous place. There is no retreating."

"Send me a message when you are coming and going with your suitcases."

"Buen día." Alexandre turns to the door.

ᏬᏬᏬ

At the end of the day, as is their habit, Alexandre and Shale meet Pat and Fred in the hotel bar for a drink. It's clear that Pat has a non-alcoholic buzz on today. Shale is hoping it is due to news from Dorothy and Sheila. She looks from Pat to Fred.

"We must go. No question. It's been too long . . . best medicine . . . fun. Anyway I've bought tickets." Pat takes a big breath.

"Tickets? Where to?" The sound of Alexandre's voice has a way of centring Pat.

"A dance party tonight. A Swing Band in the ballroom. Here! Can you believe it?"

"Now . . . is the greater mystery." Fred is sage-like. He gives Alexandre a friendly punch on the arm. "You Madrileños are a class act."

"Speaking of class," Pat adds, "we can finally dress up in those beautiful clothes we got in Paris."

"Well, our Social Secretary has spoken. We best take ourselves to the dining room for supper. We're going to need to fuel this evening" —Shale smiles at Pat — "on more than alcohol."

"Yeah, I want to be swungover, not hungover." Pat laughs hard at the look of confusion on Alexandre's face. "You'll see, old-timer."

They're all laughing as they leave the bar.

♋♋♋

The Gran Vía ballroom is more Vienna than New York. The orchestra, in black tie and tails, turns into a *Big Band* when they raise their trumpets, trombones, and saxophones. A banner hung above the band admonishes the ticket holders to KICK UP YOUR HEELS.

Pat, as the group's guide, names the dances being performed: Lindy Hop, Charleston, and Balboa. The last name is familiar to Alexandre; he's intrigued. The Balboa has the closed, chest-to-chest style of a waltz, but the rest is all fast footwork: female prance steps; male smooth slide steps, swings, quick turns. Vasco Núñez de Balboa, Spanish explorer and conquistador, would have used some fancy footwork to stay alive in the New World, but nothing like this. Alexandre's reverie is broken when Hazen Sise arrives.

Noticing the throng standing at the edge of the dance floor, the conductor takes pity, taps his wand, and directs the orchestra in a waltz.

Hazen sweeps Pat onto the dance floor. Alexandre extends a hand to Shale, their progress elegant, almost stately.

"This is a pleasant surprise," Shale says to his shoulder.

"That I can dance?"

Laughing, she pushes away to better see his face. "Of course not. I view you as an accomplished man of the world."

"What, then?"

"Irony. Just the other evening, we were in a shootout, and now we're pretending the world is civilized."

"Humans are nothing if not adaptable."

"Don't forget fickle."

He holds her at arm's-length. "You're too young to be jaded."

"But not too young to be a realist."

Alexandre looks at her closely, as if trying to decide what to say next. "You're remarkable."

Shale stops dancing, turning them into an obstacle on the crowded dance floor. She recovers with a jolt when an elbow assaults her right shoulder blade. "Perhaps we need to retire from this battlefield while we can still walk," she proposes.

"The bar, then?" Alexandre leads the way, running interference.

"Only if we can find a quiet corner."

And quiet it is: everyone, including the staff, drawn to the music.

"I apologize if I spoke out of turn. I stand by what I said, but a dance floor is hardly the place."

Shale has a mischievous glint in her eye. "Am I remarkable because I can handle a firearm and a foxtrot? Not at the same time, obviously. Although the way my shoulder feels, I'd have reason enough to use my Mauser on that oafish dancer."

Alexandre shakes with contained laughter. "You don't let anything stand in your way. Like a river . . . you flow over, under, around obstacles without pause."

"I wish that were true." Shale seems resolute.

"Of course, there is the occasional dam, but you're not diverted. Why is that?"

This is not Dr. Castro asking, she thinks—this is a friend. "Loss. When you no longer have someone to give you direction, you have no choice but to set your own course. And in doing so, there is no one to blame but yourself."

"I suspect, you learned responsibility at a very young age," he remarks.

"For better and for worse."

"Why worse?"

"Being young, you don't discriminate . . . nor do you have the power of choice." She pauses to see if he is with her. "If a burden is put on your young shoulders, you carry it. Much like the horses loaded with quarried fossils, I led down Mount Field."

"And better?" Alexandre wants both sides of the equation.

"I can choose my burdens."

"And that is why you are remarkable . . . you have the power of choice and yet you're here."

"Cowardice, really. I couldn't live with the blame I would heap on myself if I did nothing."

"You're not remarkable; you're wise . . . remarkably wise."

"I choose to accept your conclusions, if you liberate that bottle of brandy on the bar so we can have a drink in your room." Shale notes the look on his face. "I'll pay for it in the morning."

They sit in wingback chairs moved away from the heavily draped window, a tumbler each of brandy warming in their cupped hands.

"Once we finish with the vault, will you stay on in Madrid?" Shale pours words into what is suddenly an awkward moment.

"For a time. I want to work with the Committee for Protection of Spain's Treasures."

"Oh . . . great minds think alike. I plan to offer my services to the Museo Arqueológico Nacional. The Director told me the Museo is also a member of the government's National Junta for the Protection of Artistic Treasures."

"I should be here. These are my treasures to protect, my patrimony." Alexandre rises. "But you . . . things will only get worse in Madrid." He paces. "You must leave . . . you and the ladies."

"We'll leave when the treasures leave. We decided after talking to Fred. He has his finger on the pulse of this place, and believes there will be an all-out offensive by Franco in February. The Fascists will try to cut off the Valencia-Madrid road. The treasures must leave while the road is open."

"I see." Alexandre stops at the side table to refill his glass. "I expected the suitcases to leave Madrid with the four of you as soon as we had finished at University City. I have alerted Felipe. He will have a driver waiting in Marseille to take all of you and the luggage to Le Havre." He turns to her. "Can't you see . . . this is the best way?"

Shale stands, tall enough to look him in the eyes. "It is a good plan for my friends. I'll sleep nights when I know they are in London, but they will be there without me." She steps closer. "I will stay with you." Reaching out, she puts a hand on his.

Alexandre lifts his other hand to her face. He strokes her cheek. "Remarkable." He holds her close.

☙☙☙☙

The winter sun has not yet risen which means the vault is silent except for the flicker of flames and the turning of pages.

"I'm ready to pack" is all Alexandre says.

"Yes, I've finished the documents. Just a few more artifacts to wrap and place between the pages."

"I'll go now and inform Mateo. We can approach The General for an escort to help with the suitcases."

"Perhaps you could bring coffee back with your news?" Shale watches him collect yesterday's cups.

On her way to the vault to retrieve a box of Bronze Age Celtic torcs and pendant earrings, Shale's attention is arrested by the title of a report among Alexandre's documents. Leafing through *Techniques of Enhanced Interrogation*, she takes note of words such as "chekas," "secret prisons," "Surrealists," and names such as Alfonso Laurencic, Luis Bunuel, and Salvador Dali. Mention of the 1929 film *Un Chien Andalou,* directed by Bunuel and Dali, has her reading in earnest. One of the enhanced techniques used in the government's secret prisons was to open an interrogation session by showing the prisoner a scene from *Un Chien Andalou.* The scene: a close-up of a woman's face; a hand prying her eye open and slashing her eyeball with a straight razor.

As for the Frenchman, Alfonso Laurencic, he designed for the Republican government prison cells meant to create mental stress in prisoners. Laurencic's cells contained concrete beds slanted at an acute angle that made reclining impossible. Bricks were cemented to the floor of the cell in zigzag patterns; the walls painted in powerful colours to provoke agitation.

Shale drops the report back on top of the pile of documents, grateful Alexandre had escaped the clutches of the State Intelligence Service.

When Alexandre arrives back within the hour, Shale assumes The General was not available. Alexandre, being the kind of person who expects results, will be frustrated she surmises. Instead, he is sporting a wry smile as he sets the coffee cups on her table.

"Wonders never cease. The militia coming to our aid the other night when we were attacked was not by luck . . . it was Mateo's doing." He stands long enough to deliver this news.

"How is that possible?" She reaches for her coffee.

"The Head, my friend and colleague Mateo, is the liaison officer between General Kléber and the Madrid militias." Alexandre paces with his coffee.

"Well, if nothing else that might explain why the streets seemingly are deserted when we come to and from the university."

"Yes, the Moncloa-Aravaca district militia has been ordered to protect us."

"They certainly hide their intent and themselves well. I haven't spotted them."

"Nor I. But we will have a chance to meet them Christmas Eve. We've been invited to a militia dinner."

"And we must thank them. We will buy gifts. Will there be children?"

"I told Mateo you would be thrilled by the prospect. I'm glad I was right." He comes to rest with his hand on her shoulder. "You are generous."

Shale places her hand over his where it lays. This moment of accord, of knowing each other, is broken when Mateo opens the door to the vault room.

"The General is in agreement." Mateo takes in the scene. "Before the day is out, I'll have code words allowing for our safe passage, including our militia escort, through The General's patrols and sentries."

He leaves as quickly as he arrived.

They grin at one another, trying not to laugh in case Mateo hears.

And hear he would, as he sticks his head back through the door. "I forgot to tell you . . . I've spoken with The Chancellor and he has agreed to receive the suitcases and store them in his private strongroom. Oh, and we have a meeting with him next week after Christmas."

Mateo is gone before Alexandre can ask, "A meeting? About what?"

He turns to Shale. "I'm not best pleased that The Chancellor is involved. I believe he does not want the Archives to leave Spain."

♋♋♋♋

The militia barracks on Calle de Francos Rodríguez has never been such a welcoming place as it is this Christmas Eve. Rows of long tables dominate the large open room, made festive with streamers and crepe paper flowers.

Mateo meets them at the door. When he sees the packages they are carrying, he calls his wife, Daria, and their three daughters over. Mateo's wife gives Alexandre a hug, and the girls take their eye off the packages long enough to do the same.

Alexandre introduces Daria to Shale, who hands the parcels to the girls. "Cakes the hotel made for us to bring . . . Turrón, Mantecados, Marzapán, Churros and a Roscón de Reyes . . . my favourite, King Cake."

"Daria and the girls have spent a month raising funds by donation for this dinner. They even set up a coffee stand on Gran Vía." Mateo gives credit where credit is due. "And despite the food shortage, Daria's committee has worked miracles."

Daria realizes there are others waiting to enter. "Thank you so much for the cakes." She ushers the girls away from the door. "Come along, we'll put the sweets on the dessert table."

Mateo takes a quick look around the room. "Follow me—there's someone I would like you to meet." He leads the way between the rows of tables. On reaching the far end of the room, he taps a tall man on the shoulder, whose reflexes are cat fast.

Mateo steps back. "Jaime, these are General Kléber's Savants."

"Ah, yes, we call you 'The Mausers.'"

"Jaime Corredor, leader of the Moncloa-Aravaca Militia—my friends, Dr. Alexandre Castro and Dr. Shale Clifden."

"You're good shots." Corredor extends his hand.

"Thank you for taking up our fight." Shale recognizes strength when she touches his hand.

"The Fifth Columnists are the worst. Scum from the bottom of our pond."

"Well said, Jaíme. And I know something about words . . . I herd thousands upon thousands of books." Mateo's smile is cryptic.

"Vaquero or pastor?" Jaime asks.

Alexandre looks Mateo up and down. "More shepherd than cowboy."

They have a laugh at Mateo's expense and Jaime addresses Alexandre and Shale, "Be seeing you."

"Tomorrow morning before dawn, Gran Vía Hotel," Mateo reminds Jaime.

Shale regrets their early start on Christmas Day as she watches the tables being loaded with wine, tapas, soup, roasted young hen, and turkey stuffed with mushrooms. The only good thing about it is that the militiamen will be back with their families for Christmas morning.

As people take their places at the tables, a priest mounts the dais. "Welcome. Before I bless our repast, I would like to bless all of the men and women who spend their days and nights in the trenches, on the barricades, sewing uniforms, and cooking the food that gives us strength to fight on."

☙❧❦

One hour before dawn, Mateo knocks discretely on The Chancellor's door. The butler opens promptly, and bends to pick up two of the suitcases from the portico. He leads the way to the strongroom in the basement, unlocks the door and retreats.

"I take it the hour is too early for The Chancellor?" Alexandre peers into a room lined with metal doors.

"He's gone to Valencia." Mateo takes a key from his pocket.

"The new home of the government—"

"Meeting with ministers." Mateo opens a tall locker.

"Let me guess . . . Josep Renau and Jesus Hernandez?" Alexandre turns to Shale, " The Director General of Fine Arts, and the Minister of Arts and Public Instruction."

"The fate of the university?" Shale asks.

"And the University Archives." Alexandre focuses his attention on Mateo. "We'll take the suitcases to the hotel. Store them there."

"Not necessary." Mateo puts a hand on Alexandre's arm to stay him. "The Chancellor is arranging transport out of the country for the Archives."

⊙⊙⊙⊙

Alexandre and Shale arrive at the Basílica de San Francisco El Grande to find the workroom strangely silent. The Director and Pat sit with their heads together over a document.

"Such dedication, Director. Working Christmas Day." Shale nods to Pat.

"Briefly. Señorita Page and I are checking the Manifest of a shipment leaving today for Valencia. We're sending it out to take advantage of the only day the guns are silenced."

"Is there anything we can do to help?" Alexandre offers.

"Not at all."

"As it happens we have finished our work at the university and would like to volunteer our services to the Biblioteca Nacional and the Museo Arqueológico."

"Well, that's fine news. We still have a long way to go in those two institutions, especially the Biblioteca." The Director glances at the Manifest.

"If I may impose with a brief question. Does the Committee have a plan to evacuate the treasures if Valencia is besieged? And to where?" Alexandre hopes the information is not confidential.

The Director looks at him closely. "The treasures are in the twin towers of Torres de Serranos. The fortress walls have been reinforced with concrete."

"What if that's not enough?"

"Why do you ask, Dr. Castro?"

"The University Archives are to leave Spain. It seems to me

Spain's Treasures would be safer out of the country."

"You are right, Señor. As we speak, arrangements are being made to transfer Spain's Treasures to Catalonia and then to Geneva . . . . I must emphasize: If Necessary." The Director stands. "I must also impress upon all of you, that this information is sub rosa."

"Of course, understood." Alex reassures The Director.

"Pat, what time should we be back to walk you home?" Shale asks.

Before Pat can answer, The Director speaks, "Since you are here, I could take you over to the Biblioteca and the Museo to show you around. Señorita Page can finish checking the Manifest in time for our return."

The clamour has gone out of the streets of Madrid. Shale finds it pleasant to stroll and contemplate the beautiful buildings that go unnoticed in the everyday bustle. At the Biblioteca Nacional, they are greeted by San Isidoro, Alfonso El Sabio, and three other marble men, all holding books and scrolls. More than the learned statues, Shale is in awe of the three arched doors, magnificent with intricate metalwork. Once inside, her sense of precise grandeur is dispelled by a riot of books. Table after table is piled high with volumes, leather clad and voluminous. Shelves with books piled one on top of the other, makes her think of strata . . . the layers of the earth revealed to be read by archaeologists.

"As I said, there is much work to be done here. Volunteers document each book after checking its pedigree and state of health."

"Dios mío, this is who we are . . . the record of our being." Alexandre can't help but run his fingers along the closest spines.

"Not everyone thinks of books as a legacy." The Director is thoughtful. "The University Archives . . . what kind of legacy are they?"

"The Archives are both the past and the future. Scientific research that defines the human mind and body, technology that sustains the human mind and body, and culture that elevates the human mind and spirit." Alexandre weighs a large book in both hands, its blood-red cordovan leather binding worn to a warm burgundy by many hands.

"What it is to be human," Shale says across the mountains of books.

"If I can be proudly patriotic for a moment . . .. The Archives house the record of some of our greatest minds. Since 1904, three Spaniards have become Noble Prize winners. Donated to The University are the papers of José Echegaray and Jacinto Benavente, Laureates in Literature, and my mentor, Santiago Ramón y Cajal, Laureate in Medicine."

"We both bear a burden for our country. I hope it doesn't take our lives." The Director leaves the hall of books, locks the door behind them, and leads the way around the corner to the Museo Arqueológico Nacional.

A more orderly chaos greets them, with the exception of packing paper flounced everywhere like the discarded skirts of Flamingo dancers. A wooden packing crate stands beside a table, the denizens of which immediately capture Shale's attention. Residing on the table is the Lady of Elche, a finely carved bust from the fourth century BC, and keeping her company is the Bull of Osuna, her protector from the fifth century BC.

"You are familiar with these pieces, Dr. Clifden?" The Director has noticed her enthrallment.

"Yes, the beauty and the beast." Shale's smile is artful, perhaps a little arch.

Alexandre joins the mischief. "She is incredibly beautiful. Why haven't I met this exquisite creature before now? You've been remiss, Director."

"The Lady has been in purdah. Too many young men have become besotted with her. We had to take her off display. They insisted on stroking her. Eventually, all that would have been left of her stone self . . . a pebble."

Alexandre and Shale look stunned and then laugh loud enough to create echoes in the marble halls that bring the museum guards running.

∽∽∽∽

Christmas dinner in the Gran Vía Hotel dining room— although Pat is missing her family, she agrees with Alexandre and Shale that they are fortunate to have a fine meal before them. While recounting stories of home and hearth Christmas traditions, they are interrupted by the concierge with a message for Alexandre.

He takes the card and replaces it with a coin. "It's from Mateo. He would like to meet us in the hotel bar for an after-dinner drink."

"On Christmas Day?" Shale is surprised.

"Well, he is outnumbered at home. And the girls can be a handful."

"But still?"

"Yes, I think there's more to it—something he does not want to discuss at home."

Quiet descends on their feast, until Pat asks if there will be Christmas crackers with dessert?"

"Afraid not." Alexandre smiles at the thought. "Not a Spanish tradition, but it is one I enjoyed when I lived in America. Quite a merry way to begin or end a meal."

☙☙☙☙

Despite the empty glass in front of him on the bar, Mateo does not look full of Christmas cheer.

Alexandre greets him with a most untraditional hug. "You look as though Christmas dinner didn't agree with you."

"Not at all. Just wondering when there will truly be peace and joy."

Alexandre motions to the bartender. "A bottle of champagne—one with lots of noise and bubbles. We need a joyful sound."

They all laugh, including the bartender.

"Let's retire to a table." Alex heads for their regular table in the corner. "And you can tell us what's on your mind, my friend."

The bartender makes a show of opening their bottle of champagne, and placing it in an ice bucket. A waiter brings it over with a set of fine glasses. Once filled, they toast good health and long life, fully aware of the irony.

"Alexandre, The General has requested the medical supplies you brought to Madrid."

"Does he intent to treat the wounded on site at University City?"

"No. The International Brigades hospital in Huete is in dire need of medical supplies."

"Mateo, I gave everything to Dr. Bethune."

"Oh, that is unfortunate. Do you know what he's done with them?"

"No, but I can find out. I'll visit the Canadian Medical Unit tomorrow morning."

The Christmas Day exiles concentrate on their champagne and stories of Christmases spent away from home in places such as Switzerland, Norway, Mexico, and Lebanon.

While contemplating a second bottle, the concierge makes an appearance in the bar, followed by Hazen Sise.

"Well, you are in luck Mateo. This is just the man we need." Alexandre rises.

"Not just you," Pat says quietly, but not so sotto voce that Shale doesn't hear. She gives Pat a conspiratorial look.

Hazen stops at the table and glances one to the other. "Am I intruding?"

"Quite the opposite. You're the reason we're ordering a second bottle of champagne."

Hazen quickly establishes, to Mateo's relief, that the medical supplies and the ambulance are still in the compound at 36 Principe de Vergara. "I've not had a chance to do anything about distributing the supplies."

Mateo fills him in on the need at the Huete hospital.

"Brigaders, you say, a hospital for the International Brigades. Yes, of course, where the need is greatest." Hazen accepts a glass of champagne. "The thing is . . . I can't get away. We're that busy. The General will need to assign a driver."

"I'm sure that can be arranged."

Christmas day is seen out with the joyful sound of two more bottles of champagne.

Early the next morning, Alexandre and Shale arrive at the Basílica with Pat. The Director is there before them. Pat goes to her typewriter and the stack of cards beside it.

"Good morning," The Director greets them. "We'll go over to the Biblioteca and Museo now. I'll introduce you around."

Where there was only books and silence yesterday, there is now the true ambience of a library: the sound of pages turning, pens scribbling, punctuated by the occasional cough.

Alexandre has barely met the seven volunteers, been assigned a section of the bookshelves, and become engrossed in a first edition of the plays of Lope de Vega, when Mateo startles him with a touch on his shoulder. "Alexandre, I need a word . . . outside."

Alexandre's newly met bibliophiles barely notice. In the hall, Mateo moves toward an alcove that leads to the stone balcony above the main entrance. "The Chancellor sent me to tell you that he has arranged passage on a ship for the suitcases."

"Not without—"

"You. Yes, I know Alexandre. The passage includes you, Dr. Clifden, and her friends."

"When?"

"One week from today. The ship departs from Valencia, docking in Marseille. The time is right. The General has received word that the Nationalists plan to launch an offensive to take the Valencia-Madrid Road on February sixth."

"Transportation?" Alexandre has taken on Mateo's brisk tone.

"You can drive your ambulance and the medical supplies to Huete. You'll have an escort. Then travel to Albacete, collect Miss Livesay and Miss Doherty, find a driver, and take the ambulance on to Valencia. Josep Renau will meet with you there."

"Well, The Chancellor works in mysterious ways."

"When will you leave?"

"As soon as possible. There's bound to be problems on the road, even with a military escort."

"Yes. Spain is divided and with it lawless. A shining example is the Fascist priest in Villanueva de la Jara, who climbed the steps to the church bell tower toting a machine gun and cut down his parishioners in the square below."

"In my professional opinion, clergy are prime candidates for psychoses."

"You truly are a man of science."

"Mateo, I'll see you before I leave Madrid. And thank you. Your help has meant the world."

℥℥℥

"Calm before the storm" is how Shale characterizes the Valencia-Madrid Road to Huete. The General's troop truck, destined to pick up international soldiers from Albacete, garners them a certain respect from the few vehicles they pass. Even the fields and villages seem deserted; they surmise the inhabitants have fled to the mountains.

In Huete, Alexandre parks the ambulance in front of a crumbling stone building that has the look of a monastery. The arrival of the medical supplies has caused a stir in the largely nursing staff of the makeshift hospital. New Zealand nurses Millicent Sharples, René Shadbolt, and Isobel Dodds take over the unloading of the ambulance. Shale and Pat are shunted aside, while Alexandre goes to speak with the hospital's commander.

A heavy Renault truck pulls into the driveway at speed, braking hard. A woman jumps out of the driver's side, shouting in Spanish at the unloading crew.

Shale steps into the driver's path as she descends on the nurses. "Qué está pasando?"

Pat joins her.

The driver recognizes a non-Spanish speaking interlocutor. "You're American, right?"

"Canadian," Pat says. "And Canadian-American."

"Whoever you are, move that vehicle right now. I've got wounded."

"Won't be long. We're unloading medical supplies."

The driver looks at them closely and as she does, her eyes widen. "Dorothy's friends . . . you're Dorothy's friends, aren't you?"

"Who are you?" Pat asks, shocked.

"Jean Watts."

"I'll be damned; Dorothy found you." Pat advances, hand out. "How are Dorothy and Sheila? Are they all right?"

Alexandre leaves the hospital in time to move the unloaded ambulance. Jean pulls the Renault truck up to the entrance. Alexandre lifts the tarp at the back and signals to their escort to come and help unload the wounded.

Back on the road, they form a convoy with the troop truck in the lead and Jean Watts's Renault bringing up the rear. The driver of the troop truck avoids the Valencia-Madrid Road with its increase in military traffic as they travel south.

The convoy comes to a halt on the infamous square of Villanueva de la Jara. The village church looms large. Reluctant to leave the protection of the ambulance, they simply stare.

Jean thumps on the ambulance roof with her fist. "Suppertime, you must be hungry. Everyone will be in the mess hall."

"Why are we stopping here?" Alexandre asks Jean through the open driver's side window. "We could make Albacete before dark."

"Albacete, bah . . .. Brigade Headquarters is in the Gran Hotel Albacete Castilla-La Mancha. That should tell you everything you need to know. Jara is the base of operations. This is where all the training takes place and the boys are deployed to the front."

Pat wastes no time getting out of the ambulance. "That means Dorothy and Sheila are here, right?"

"They'll be in the church." Jean starts across the square.

Shale catches her up. "I thought you said the mess?"

"Yeah, in the church hall. Food's decent, too."

Pat spots Dorothy and Sheila sitting with two young men. "Hey, you," she shouts across the hall. All heads turn, but it is only Dorothy and Sheila who jump to their feet.

"What?"

"What are you doing here?"

"Obviously, rescuing you from those two." Pat nods at her friends' supper companions and smiles.

"They're Canadian" is all Sheila can think to say.

"All right, then . . .." Shale gives Sheila a hug.

"We've come to collect you. We're leaving Spain." Alexandre is shaking hands and patting shoulders.

"Leaving?" Dorothy is startled.

"We have passage on a ship from Valencia to Marseille in two days time." He realizes they are disconcerted. They have become accustomed to Jara. Not for the first time he marvels at how adaptable these young women are.

Dorothy glances at the Canadian volunteers who seem

bewildered by the new arrivals. "Come meet our new friends."
She grabs Pat's hand.

Introductions are buffeted by the rising noise in the mess hall as
trays of food are laid out on side tables and a long hatch is opened
to reveal the kitchen and its staff.

Finally, Dorothy takes charge. "Let's have a picnic. Grab what
you can, and we'll find a place in the pine forest." The Canadians,
Thomas Beckett and Larry Ryan, salute and charge the food tables.

Carrying their bounty, the troop climbs a slope behind the church
that leads away from the village. Accosted by the cool fragrance of
black pine, they enter a world removed.

"Siete," Dorothy says.

"You mean 'sentarse,' don't you, Miss Livesay?" Alexandre looks
around for a place to sit.

"No, we call this grove . . . Seven."

"There are many more pines than seven."

"Group of Seven . . . our little joke. Canadian landscape painters
from the Algonquin School who like to paint pictures of trees."
Thomas Beckett is grinning at his audience. "Just a way to feel
at home."

"Have you been in Spain long?" Shale asks.

"Not long, but I've lost count of the days."

"Why did you leave the Land of the White Pine?" Shale sits
with her back against a fallen tree.

"Because I wasn't heard in Canada . . . couldn't make a difference."
Thomas Beckett sits beside her.

Dorothy takes up a place on Shale's other side. "Thomas was the
chairman of a unit of the Toronto Co-operative Commonwealth
Federation. But that wasn't enough . . . was it Thomas? Didn't matter
whether you rode a freight train across Canada to confront the
government in Ottawa or demonstrated on Parliament Hill . . . the
fat cat politicians have got their hands over their ears."

Thomas looks across Shale. "I could have used you at the
rallies, Dorothy."

"Next time. When we get home. Promise."

Shale looks from one to the other, and then at Alexandre. Her
expression is soft, open, tender.

Sheila has not missed the nuance of the exchange.

"And how is it you've come to be in Spain, Mr. Ryan?" Shale attempts to be inclusive.

"It's Jim's fault." Larry points at Jean Watts.

"But you came with Thomas . . . you're both from Toronto." Sheila touches his arm to divert his attention from Jean.

"Yes, but Jim woke me up. Her articles in the *Daily Clarion*, you know, the Canadian Communist Party newspaper."

"Jim?" Pat looks around. "Whose Jim?"

Jean laughs. "Me. It's what they call me here."

"Why?"

"Because she's a great mechanic," Thomas speaks up before Larry can. "As well as an ambulance driver."

"You want something fixed, Jim's your . . . grease monkey." Larry lowers his eyes, then laughs.

"Well, now that's settled—" Dorothy is interrupted by the sound of a bugle.

"That's us." Thomas stands. "We're being called to the training grounds."

"Good to meet you. Got to gallop. Never pays to be late around here. They're sticklers." Larry is already on the path.

Alexandre turns to Jean. "Would you be willing to drive us to Valencia? And bring the ambulance back?"

"You'll have to talk to the commander." Jean is tentative.

"Yes, of course, I just don't want him to assign anyone else. I'm sure he'll be amenable, since I'm donating the ambulance to the Brigades."

"I see. Well, I certainly would like more time with all of you. And what better way than a road trip." Jean loops her arm through Alexandre's. "Let's go talk to him now."

The others, making no attempt to leave the sanctuary of the pines, watch them go.

Pat turns to Sheila. "Did you give them what for . . . on the training grounds?"

"Those boys," Dorothy answers for the abashed Sheila. "When she left the Women's Militia to train with the volunteers, some of those boys snickered, most were condescending . . . until they got on the rifle range. Sheila put them to shame."

"No great feat," Sheila explains. "They're mostly city boys. Never handled anything more than a toy gun."

"I bet you filed some crackerjack dispatches, right?" Pat is eager to hear about their deeds.

"No complaints from The Canadian Press," Dorothy sums up their work in Jara. She wants to move on. "So, you got the Archives out of Madrid?"

Pat is disappointed. "Alexandre and Shale filled our suitcases. They're in the ambulance."

"And so, we're leaving . . . what if we don't want to go?" Dorothy studies Sheila.

"Up to you, I guess. No one can make you," Pat offers. "But we've been told the fighting is going to get worse really soon. The Italian Blackshirts are crossing from Morocco to Málaga on the Mediterranean, and the Condor Legion has been sent from Germany. What can you two do to make a difference against shock troops and bomber squadrons?" Pat stands rooted to the ground, a grim expression on her young face.

ରେଉେ

The ambulance is a tight squeeze front and back, but no one seems to mind, not even Alexandre pressed hard against the passenger's door with Sheila between him and Jean at the wheel. He's got the window open, the wind muffling the sound of the women singing popular songs. He has to admit it has brought them around after the drunken farewell party last night. It would appear Dorothy and Sheila had made an impression on the volunteers. The men had adopted the two of them as mascots. The evening ended with Dorothy and Sheila sitting in chairs placed either side of the mess hall door and the men parading by, each touching the heads of the young women for luck. Dorothy and Sheila murmuring all the while, "Come home". . . a kind of blessing.

Alexandre glances into the backseat and notices that Shale is scouring the landscape. At first, he thinks she is being their scout.

Although Jean has decided on a route through the backcountry and away from the Valencia-Madrid Road, there is still considerable traffic – sadly, people fleeing their homes.

"Shale, have you spotted any bandits?" Alexandre must shout above a rendition of *Pennies From Heaven*.

"Not here, not in the Sierra Martés, too rugged," Jean answers his question.

"Caves," Shale says. "There are caves in these mountains dating from the Chalcolithic period. Copper . . . metalworking in copper, before someone discovered that by adding tin, you could make bronze."

"That's right." Jean glances in the rear-view mirror. "You lured my friend to Spain with talk of archaeology—one of the more romantic of the new sciences. Certainly, more so than psychology. I failed to become a doctor, but I have a degree in psychology from the University of Toronto."

Shale flashes Alexandre a look, curious as to his response to Jean's declaration.

"It appears, Miss Watts, that we are fellow travellers."

This is Alexandre being circumspect, Shale thinks.

"Oh, indeed. How so? Other than this dusty road through scrub pine."

"I also have degrees in the young science of psychology. I was instrumental in establishing the Psychology Department at the University of Madrid."

"I have to say, my studies have become useful, especially when I'm required to provide transportation for those soldiers whose minds have been shattered along with their bodies."

"Oh, Gina, what you must see here. Will you ever be the same?" Dorothy has tears in her eyes.

"None of us will be." Jean examines the backseat in the dash mirror. "Nor should we be."

ᏋᏋᏋᏋ

The smell of the sea rushes in the open windows before the city appears on the horizon.

Alexandre is alerted. "Jean. Do you know the Bank of Valencia?"

"Is that where we're going?"

"Yes, arrangements have been made for us to store the Archives there overnight."

Sometime later, Jean pulls up in front of an ornate building.

"My gosh, this can't be a bank . . . it looks like a wedding cake." Pat is entranced.

"Beautiful . . . classic columns . . . a cupola that could serve as a temple." Dorothy seems to be talking to herself.

"I'll find us some parking." Jean, as driver, is focused on necessity not beauty.

"Let me out at the entrance, if you would, Jean, and I'll make our arrival known." Alexandre is all business.

"In that case, I'll simply wait here for you."

Alexandre reappears shortly. "They are ready for us. We have permission to park and unload here."

Suitcases in hand, the women create something of an impression when they enter the bank's rotunda. Alexandre is grateful to Shale, who purchased a small leather trunk in Madrid and filled it with the SHE Gang's best clothes. A humorous thought flits across his mind . . . the ladies could be gangsters' molls, as portrayed in the American crime movies he frequented when he was at Harvard.

A clerk leads them down a hall lined with vault doors. He stops at one that is open, displaying an inner door made of steel bars. He unlocks it and directs the women inside. He gestures for them to pile the suitcases on a low shelf. To Alexandre, he says, "The President awaits you in his office. He has telephoned Director General Renau and is pleased to offer refreshments while you wait.

The bank president's windows look out over the city centre, equally as grandiose as his office. The man himself is rotund and corpulent, in keeping with his position. He rises to greet his guests as described by the Director General, with the exception of one young woman dressed in dungarees and a man's shirt.

The formalities are barely uttered when the office door opens and Josep Renau is announced. Introductions take place over coffee this time. Whereas the President's attention is on Dr. Castro, the

Director General is talking politics with Jean Watts, and he is fully aware she is a newspaper reporter before an ambulance driver.

The sun makes a pronouncement on the day through the arched bank windows. "Are you familiar with the city?" Renau asks the group.

"Tangentially, Director General," Alexandre replies. "I have conferred with colleagues here occasionally."

"I also have colleagues at the Universitat de València, met primarily through correspondence." Shale turns to the others with an obvious invitation to speak.

Among the shaking of heads, Jean is the only one to contribute, "I make frequent trips to Valencia, transporting critically wounded soldiers to the Pasionaria Military Hospital."

"I have a proposal," Renau focuses on his guests. "I will be your tour guide, while we walk to your hotel."

The President looks on in astonishment.

"What of our vehicle?" Jean asks.

"I will have my assistant remove it to the hotel compound."

ଚ୨ଚ୨ଚ୨

Josep Renau, standing like an orator on the bank's stairs between the bank's classical columns, with a sweeping gesture, claims the city as his own. He is a son of Valencia.

The Director General takes his job as tour guide seriously; his running commentary is instructive. He leads them into a street hung not with banners but huge posters—an outdoor gallery. They stop at each one as he provides a translation and expands on the art and letters. What the posters have in common is graphic violence: *The Final Blow Must Be Struck* . . . HAY QUE DAR EL GOLPE DEFINITIVO. A muscular revolutionary rendered head to toe in red stands on the neck of a fantastical snake, its fanged mouth open, revealing a tongue tipped with the Nazi swastika. The man in worker's clothes wields an axe.

"This painting is the work of Valencia artist, Sanz Miralles. It was commissioned by the Anarchist Union."

The next poster is apocalyptic, revealing the impetus behind Spain's catastrophic conflict: *Land Worker. The revolution will give you land* . . . *Campesino. la revolución te dará la tierra*. Yet another muscular red man, this time impaling on the end of his rife bayonet a boar-like monster in top hat and tails, dagger in hand. The capitalist monster and the farmer-militiaman confront each other on a chunk of earth in the shape of the Iberian Peninsula.

The tour ends with the largest of the posters: *Land Worker Defend With Weapons The Government That Will Give You Land* . . . *CAMPESINO DEFIENDE CON LAS ARMAS AL GOBIERNO QUE TE DIO LA TIERRA*. What is different about this muscular red man with rifle raised, a serpent entwining its length until run through by the bayonet, is that the poster is signed Renau.

The onlookers are surprised with the exception of Shale. She has followed the career of the artist, critic, and political activist Josep Renau since she first became aware of two phrases associated with him: "Re-imagining the nation" and "Ethics through aesthetics." His cultural programs promoting democracy through the belief that art must be delivered to the people were put into practice with the Pedagogical Missions of 1931.

Shale contemplates the poster. "Señor Director, it seems to me this is another instance of ethics through aesthetics."

Renau's astonished countenance gives Shale a slight tickle along her spine. She makes a pronouncement, "The Misiones Pedagógicas were a brave initiative. Republican in the true sense of the word."

"Thank you, Dr. Clifton. That is gratifying to hear. Especially in this time and place."

They walk on.

The Director General's driver has parked in front of their hotel. Before Director Renau departs, he hands Alexandre a large envelope: "Your travel documents. The ship leaves tomorrow at noon for Marseille. God speed."

The hotel bar, out of step with the buildings of Valencia, is classical rather than sumptuous. A room of elegant restraint with traditional cordovan leather chairs, dark wood tables, and antique tapestries warming the walls.

The women take on the look of their surroundings: they are restrained when they should be jubilant. They drink in silence, each contemplating the turbulent time they have spent in Spain, each wondering about home. The exception is Jean, who downs her drink, and calls for another round by banging her glass repeatedly on the table. It gets everyone's attention. "So, you're going home, eh?" She looks around the table.

"Can we go home?" Dorothy continues to contemplate her drink.

"Why can't we?" Pat is alarmed.

"We can, but will we? Are we really done here, or are we abandoning Spain?" Dorothy glances across at Alexandre.

"There is still work to do," he says.

"For you, yes. The Archives must be secured with the Smithsonian."

Since it is her lifelong friend raising these questions, Jean decides to speak up, "Come back to Jara with me, Dorothy."

Dorothy is startled, as are the others by Jean's request. The waiter arrives with a tray of drinks, breaking the tension.

It is clear Dorothy is on the verge of tears. "I don't have your fighting spirit, Gina. We've always known that. Your aggressiveness will keep you alive here and sane. Remember, I'm the poet and you're the firebrand."

"Then write. But not from home. Stay in Europe and put that mighty brain of yours to work for the gallant cause."

Sheila raises her fist in the Republican salute. "Here, here! And I mean: Here."

Alexandre survey's the bar and its staff, searching for signs of any unusual interest in their table.

A few more drinks, and Jean is posing personal questions to her drinking companions:

"Pat aren't you rather young to be loose in the big world?"

"Sheila, where did you learn how to shoot like a sniper?"

"Shale, Alexandre . . . are you two a couple? You got something going on here?"

The next day, Jean doesn't remember the questions, let alone the answers.

꩜꩜꩜

Standing in front of the Bank of Valencia's grand doors is the bank president's assistant. The bank has yet to open; the assistant leads them to a side entrance.

Inside, they collect the suitcases from the vault. The assistant leads them to a meeting room on the third floor, where coffee awaits, as does the President. He addresses Shale, "Dr. Clifden, I have an interest in archaeology, and it would give me great pleasure to view the artifacts under your guardianship."

"With pleasure." Shale retrieves her suitcase and lays it on the conference table.

She has barely unwrapped a few pieces when there is an almighty noise from the street below, dominated by blaring trumpets and beating drums.

The assistant hastily unlocks a set of double doors opening on to a wrought iron balcony. The oblong bank building faces down a wide avenue that is alive with marching soldiers. At the sound of a bugle, fists are raised in salute. The soldiers wear side caps and shoulder-to-hip sashes in the form of folded-and-tied woolen blankets. Rifles rest smartly on padded shoulders.

Citizens stream to the sidewalks to cheer on the parade. A roar goes up when a group of men appear at the end of the ranks, dressed in an assortment of uniforms from the Great War and carrying Canadian Expeditionary Force Ross rifles. It is clear–Jean cheers loudly–that this is a contingent of volunteers from Villanueva de la Jara.

Alexandre looks on, concerned by the ever-growing number of people packing the parade route, and yet, entranced by the sense of purpose radiating from soldiers and citizens.

Finally, he manages to get Jean's attention. He points to his watch.

Jean shouts, "We got to go. With this throng, I don't know how I'll get you to the docks. You got to make that ship."

The President grasps the situation. "My assistant can guide you through the side streets. If you have room for him."

"Thanks," Jean says. "We'll make room."

After a zigzag dash through the centre of Valencia, Jean pulls up dockside in time to witness International Volunteers marching down the gangplank of the ship her friends are meant to board. The group unload the suitcases and say their goodbyes in a swirl of men speaking many different languages. The world has been called to Valencia.

In an attempt to marshall the mob, a man standing in the back of a troop truck shouts through a megaphone, "It is better to die on your feet than to live on your knees."

A chant of "La Pasionaria, La Pasionaria" echoes off the sides of the looming ships.

EPILOGUE

EXPOSITION INTERNATIONALE
DES ARTS ET TECHNIQUES
DANS LA VIE MODERNE

PARIS 1937

Shale and Alex stand shoulder to shoulder at the second-floor railing of the Eiffel Tower. They have climbed the innumerable flights of steel stairs to gain a bird's-eye view of the Exposition Internationale. Facing the Seine, Alexandre takes a site map from his leather satchel, and once unfolded, they attempt to match the pavilions marked on the map to the buildings below them. They are familiar with those pavilions at the feet of the grand tower, especially Canada's constructed from rotund concrete columns reminiscent of grain silos and dominated by a twenty-eight-foot sculpture of a buffalo that has beguiled Shale.

As the tall fashionable couple gazes across the Seine, they are confronted by the towering German and Soviet pavilions, topped with massive sculptures. Dominating the Soviet stepped tower of stone are two striding workers brandishing a hammer and a sickle. Germany's edifice is guarded by an eagle with a Swastika breastplate. Nazi Germany and the Soviet Union face each other across a reflecting pond and strike aggressive stances, casting dark shadows over the pavilions of their European neighbours. An ill wind lifts the map from Alexandre's hands and it flies away, as does Shale's white straw boater.

Before the map took flight, they had located the Spanish Pavilion. And an earlier boat trip up the Seine to the Eiffel Tower plaza had given them a fish-eye view of a dozen pavilions and state buildings.

Alexandre laughs. "I hope the map lands on the Canadian Pavilion and not some unsuspecting pedestrian."

"The way it's dipping and diving, it could swoop across the river and peck the Nazi eagle right on the swastika. Or cover the genitals of the naked German statues with their unashamed posturing."

"And where will your hat land?" Alexandre is grinning at Shale's flight of fancy.

"On the head of the Soviet woman worker. She can wear it while she cuts down wheat or dissenters with her sickle."

Pressed against the iron railing, they look out over an engineered world. Shale lifts her arm and sweeps the view away. "This is not a celebration of modern life . . . it is an exposition of power."

Later, after a harrowing climb down the Eiffel Tower stairs, a leisurely walk across the Pont d'Iéna, and then around the reflecting pond, Alexandre and Shale stand before a house of glass that invites the world to witness Spain's betrayal and sorrow.

Alexandre reads aloud, translating into English, the plaque on a stone sculpture the height of the three-storey ultra-modern pavilion, "*The Spanish people have a path that leads to a star.*"

The statue seems like an elongated arm to Shale. "It's a torturous path. Look, the statue is reflected in the photomural of Republican soldiers over the entrance."

Immediately, they understand the purpose of the Spanish Pavilion. On entering the main floor, they expect propaganda, but not in the form of Spanish artist Joan Miró's two-storey abstract mural, *The Reaper*: a Catalan peasant in revolt with clenched fist, raised sickle, and wearing the banned barretina—a hat symbolizing Catalan identity. *The Reaper* is meant to prepare them to be overwhelmed, if not by Picasso's *Guernica*, than by the toxic fumes of Alexander Calder's *Mercury Fountain*.

Turning to the stairs that rise to the second floor, Shale and Alexandre come face-to-face with *La Pasionaria*—a black-and-white photo of Dolores Ibárruri, the conscience of Spain, superimposed on a painting of a raised fist, framed by passionflowers, and surmounted by a photo of a microphone. The red banner at the bottom reads, "Better to be the widow of a hero than the wife of a coward. No Pasarán." The photomontage is signed by Josep Renau.

The second-floor gallery displays Josep Renau photomurals of Spanish life before and after—women in traditional dress, and women fleeing destruction, clutching infants to their naked breasts. A prelude to Picasso's visceral response to the April bombing of Guernica, a town in Basque Country, the heart of Basque culture and northern Spain's Republican resistance. A terror bombing by the Nazi Germany Condor Legion was planned for a market day when women and children would be in the centre of town. The air raid destroyed the town in two hours by unloading one thousand-pound bombs and aluminum incendiary projectiles. Those citizens hiding in the fields outside Guernica were strafed with machine gunfire.

Leaving the second floor by the spiral staircase, Shale and Alexandre are ambushed. The SHE Gang is waiting for them, directed there by the ringleader, Josep Renau. The reunion is jubilant, the young women in high spirits.

"You're here, we're here!" Pat is bouncing up and down on her toes like a nervous ballerina. "What could be better?"

"Champagne! After all, it is Paris."

They stare at Renau in surprised anticipation.

"We have bottles on hand for just such occasions. Follow me."

Renau gathers up bottles and glasses with the help of Pat and Sheila. He leads them outdoors to a small private courtyard at the back of the pavilion.

Raising his glass, Alexandre toasts the Spanish Pavilion, "A tribute to art in the service of reality."

"Hear, hear! I'll drink to that." Dorothy downs her flute of champagne.

"And here's to a new reality for Shale and Alexandre. Congratulations!" Renau is alone in raising his glass. His eyes shift between the subjects of his toast and the young women.

"Thank you, Josep, for celebrating our marriage." Shale's focus is on the SHE Gang.

"I knew it. I told you so." Pat flings herself at Shale.

The rejoicing in the courtyard drowns out the sound of explosions and gunfire coming from the pavilion's auditorium, where the documentary films *España 1936* and *The Spanish Earth* are being shown.

Renau refills glasses, as Alexandre opens the satchel at his feet and Shale helps him lift out leather-bound books. The title is rendered in gold leaf, BE BRAVE: CONFRONTING THE PRIMITIVE IN SPAIN 1936–1937.

Pat is less interested in the books than she is in Alexandre's and Shale's hands laying the volumes out across the table. "Where are your wedding rings?"

"We plan to have rings made here in Paris," Shale explains. "We took off our temporary bands in order to surprise you."

"Well, you succeeded," Dorothy observes. "It would seem that America was good for you."

"Very." Shale smiles. "Besides a lovely intimate wedding ceremony at the Smithsonian, I had time to write up my field notes from the SHE Cave, tackle a scholarly paper on my findings, and write the Preface for our gift of appreciation." She lifts one of the books from the table. "Be Brave is a reproduction of your notebooks, including the drawings and the diagrams. The Smithsonian publisher was enthralled with your observations and more than happy to print and bind these volumes. Thank you for being our friends and colleagues. And for the work you've done on my behalf and Spain's."

"Indeed, may I add my voice on behalf of the people of Spain: Our boundless gratitude . . . Nuestra ilimitada gratitud." Josep Renau raises his glass. "I am well aware of the work you are currently undertaking in London with the Spanish Medical Aid Committee and the Spanish Women's Committee for Help in Spain."

Shale nods in agreement. "We sent copies of Be Brave to a

number of universities in North America and Europe. There is considerable interest in the SHE Cave." Shale toasts her intrepid friends. "You've made a difference."

The moment, although tearful, is filled with the sound of droning aircraft and screaming men, women, children and animals— as if Picasso's Guernica hanging in the gallery had come alive.

"The Spanish Earth." Renau acknowledges the intrusion. "The film. Do you know it?"

They shake their heads rather than trying to make themselves heard over the soundtrack.

Renau holds up his finger. "Soon."

The scene plays out, and Renau is able to speak and be heard. "A group of American writers formed a company called Contemporary Historians Inc. to back the Dutch filmmaker Joris Ivens."

"Who are the Contemporary Historians?" Sheila asks. "Could they be the writers I met with Fred Griffin in Madrid?"

"Certainly. Ernest Hemingway and John Dos Passos . . . they were fixtures in Madrid. And perhaps Dorothy Parker, Lillian Hellman, and Archibald MacLeish. Orson Wells does the narration."

"So, it's a polemic?" Dorothy asks.

"If you mean a propaganda film . . . yes and no. It's meant to support the Republican forces and the International Brigades, while creating a pictorial record of the peoples' fight for the land of Spain and the fruits of their labour."

As if on cue the film ends abruptly. Josep Renau's eyes light up. "Oh, I had almost forgotten . . . the children's choir is performing today in the auditorium. Let's open another bottle of champagne, shall we?"

The choir mistress introduces the first selection, "The Internationale."

The young voices reach beyond the walls: "Stand up, damned of the Earth! / Stand up, prisoners of starvation! / Reason thunders in its volcano, / This is the eruption of the end. / Of the past, let us make a clean slate. / Enslaved masses, stand up stand up! / The world is about to change its foundations. / We are nothing, let us be all."

El Final

AUTHOR'S NOTE

THE PRIMITIVES is set in Spain from September 1936 to January 1937. By this time ordinary Canadians with no family ties to Spain are fighting and dying on Spanish soil, while my Canadian protagonists 'race' to save the art, artifacts and archives housed in Madrid.

World events echo my words.

"Canadian volunteers prepare to join fight against Russian invasion in Ukraine" (*CBC News, March 2, 2022*).

"Ukrainians in race to save cultural heritage" (*The Guardian, March 11, 2022*).

"University of Alberta initiative aims to protect Ukrainian archives, research" (*CBC News March 15, 2022*).